The Destitute

THE DESTITUTE

T. R. Hawes Jr.

Libary of Congress Control Number:		2009909269
ISBN:	Hardcover	978-1-4415-7336-0
	Softcover	978-1-4415-7335-3

This book was printed in the United States of America.

To order additional copies of this book, contact:
Xlibris Corporation
1-888-795-4274
www.Xlibris.com
Orders@Xlibris.com

54224

DEDICATION

This book is dedicated to my father, Terry R. Hawes Sr., who always wanted to write a novel but never seemed to get around to it. I hope you are reading it in heaven.

Acknowledgments

A special thank you to Stewart P. Evans and Keith Skinner for their book titled "The Ultimate Jack the Ripper Companion," from which valuable information was obtained.

Much obliged to Webster's dictionary for the correct words needed.

A special thank you to my dear friend Charles (Chuck) Harman for taking the author photograph.

Thank you to Virginia Baker for writing her first novel "Jack Knife," which helped inspire me to write my first novel.

Chapter One

It was 2:00 a.m.—one of the coolest mornings in Niagara Falls. Jill was standing at 18th and Cleveland Avenue, waiting for the next passing car, so maybe she could get warm, besides conduct a little business in the process. Headlights approached and pulled up alongside her. The passenger window rolled down, and a young black male smiled and said "Hey baby, whaddup?" Jill peered inside the vehicle, noticed three other males, and replied "Need some company?" "That all depends on the dead presidents, you know what I mean, baby?" he replied. "Yea, I get the picture, and that all depends on if you have a badge or not, do you get the picture? Are you the police?" "Look it, bitch, we ain't no pigs and this ain't no bacon wagon, all right?" "OK," Jill said, "it'll be $20.00 dead presidents each in advance." The man started laughing and said, "We will give $15.00 total, and we'll even throw in some Mickey D's. The others joined in the laughter, pounding fists with one another. Jill looked around and said "Hit the road, boys, this ain't welfare." Unaccustomed to being shot down, the car pulled away as obscenities were shouted back at her. Jill thought a moment, maybe she should have taken them up on their offer, since she would have gotten warm and Mickey D's was open all night. However, her declining seemed to keep her safe—she figured they were trouble.

John's carriage rolled up Eighteenth Street near Ontario Avenue, and he noticed Jill walking the other side. He instructed his driver whose name was Angus to pull up next to her. The carriage pulled up to Jill and the door opened. "Come here, love," John said. Jill turned, looked inside amidst the fog, and replied, "Who is this, calling love?" "Please step inside—it is cold outside," John said. Jill stepped inside the carriage and sat across from John. She looked at him—his curious smile and pleasant face. He seemed to her to be a little eccentric, but on the other hand a man she may be able to do business with. A certain kind of client—a rich client. A man with a carriage like this can't be all that terrible, so with that she decided to break the ice. "What can I do for you, love?" she asked. "First of all, let's get acquainted," he replied. "My name is John, and I hail from London. And you are, madam?" he inquired as he held out his hand. "My name is Jill," said she as she held out her hand. John grasped it lightly and bent down and gave it a little kiss. Jill looked down at his kiss on her hand and thought to herself, "Wow, a gentleman. These are not found around here these days." John looked back at her and said, "What a pretty name. It fits the same pretty face." "Thank you," she said back. "You are most welcome, my dear" he returned in kind. Their eyes met, and the mesmerizing stare from his dark eyes buried deep into her soul. She seemed to be hypnotized by his gaze. Then he reached into his vest pocket, brought out a snuff box, and offered her a snort. She accepted the powder, thinking it was cocaine and it was time to get high. Jill took a pinch in each nostril, sending the drug into her brain, endorphins racing all around, her body reacting violently and then all was quiet. She lay still—not dead, but in a state of unconscious euphoria. The carriage pulled into a parking area next to the closed K&J auto shop, between South and Cleveland avenues. John stared at Jill and lightly caressed her face. "You are a beautiful creature, and I must set you free of your miserable existence. Good-bye, my darling."

Chapter Two

Lt. Neil Woodredge was a ten-year veteran of the Niagara Falls Police Department, or rather was until his suspension for a shoot-and-kill of a drug dealer named Ace Johnson. Six months ago, Edge—as he liked to be called—was staking out an area on Highland Avenue near College Avenue. His unmarked was sitting across a popular night spot, and Edge was waiting for Ace to come out. He noticed Ace in front of the Elks lodge, walking in his direction. A woman named Doris Walker stopped Ace and an exchange was made. Edge made his move and radioed for backup. Ace continued making deals, when he noticed marked cars coming in both directions. Edge jumped from his vehicle, weapon drawn, and a chase ensued. Edge followed Ace, yelling for him to stop, identifying himself as a police officer. Ace kept running until he ran into a patrol car, which had doubled back, blocking his progress. Ace had Edge behind him and the patrol officer in front. "Stop, Ace," police officer Edge commanded. Ace whirled around with a weapon in his hand, pointing it at Edge. He squeezed off one shot before Edge fired twice. Ace's shot missed its target, but Edge's shots both hit Ace in the chest, exploding his heart. He was dead before he hit the ground. Edge walked over with patrolman Atkins, kicked the gun away, checked Ace's pulse, and shook his head slightly to indicate it was no use to call the paramedics. Officer Atkins walked to his patrol car to get the crime scene tape and first aid kit; just in case there might be a chance Ace might be alive. Edge radioed for a bus to transport Ace. Capt. Arthur Eckersley arrived to get the statements from any witnesses and police officers.

Criminal investigator Charlie Mort showed up with his team to gather evidence. "Hey Edge, where's Ace's gun?" Charlie asked. "It is right there, a little way from the body," Edge replied. Edge walked over to where it was last seen, and it was gone. "It was right here, where I kicked it. Someone must have taken it while we were at our cars," Edge said. Charlie looked over Edge's shoulder as the captain was approaching. "Oh shit, here comes Eckersley." Eckersley looked at Edge and down at Ace's body. "It seems we are missing something, aren't we, Edge," Eckersley said in a sarcastic tone. "The gun's missing, skipper," Edge said. "It was here—someone must have taken it." "We believe you, Lieutenant," Eckersley said with a smirk on his face. "Gotta have the badge and gun, Woodredge, until IAD clears you." Edge handed over both to the captain. As the captain walked away, he heard the lieutenant yell out, "The name's Edge."

That's how it went six months ago, and Edge had been on suspension ever since. Eckersley had been enjoying every minute of it. Edge and Eckersley never hit it off from the very start, since Edge called Eckersley CaptainClown of the station. Edge sat on his bed, thinking about the shooting and wishing it had gone another way. He couldn't figure out where the doggone gun went. A crowd showed up after the fact; it could have been anyone there. He fell back on the bed, trying to remember faces in the crowd, but no one face came to mind. His thoughts were interrupted by a knock at the door. Peeping thru the hole, he noticed Detective Abigail Cook on the other side. She was a seasoned detective and a good friend, but he didn't need any bullshit right now.

Edge opened the door and Abbie stepped in, closing the door behind her. She started the conversation, "Captain wants us down at the station, OK Edge?" "Let me get a shower, and I'll meet you there," Edge replied. "I got a better idea. Why don't we both get a shower and go together," she came back. She figured to brighten his day with her in the shower also; after all, he was her man. They had been an item for about three years now, but came slightly apart when his suspension became effective. He wasn't talking much and became very distant. Hoping there was good news today, maybe they could resume their partnership. Normally after their showers and much lovemaking, getting dressed was difficult because they wanted to keep the sex going while they were both horny. They had to get back to the station before the captain got suspicious, because, stupid as it seemed, it was the city's policy that intimate officers couldn't be partners. They got into the car and headed for the station.

Chapter Three

Capt. Arthur Eckersley was a big man—probably seen too many twinkies in his day—and stood six feet three inches tall at about 260 pounds. A stern man, but not fond of Edge one bit. He thought Edge was a loose cannon, but a good detective nonetheless. Edge was not a very controllable man; always wanted to do the law his way. Captain Eckersley heard a commotion in the squad room and noticed Edge and Abbie had arrived for the meeting. Other detectives were welcoming them. "Welcome back, Lieutenant," said Detective Reyes. "Who says I'm back. I just came in to put a bug up the captain's ass," Edge smiled at him. "That's the scuttlebutt," Reyes retorted. Entering the captain's office, Edge stood off balance in front of Eckersley. Abbie was beside him. "Detective Cook, you are dismissed," said the captain. "Thank you, sir," Abbie said as she left. "Sit down, Woodredge," Eckersley ordered. Edge pulled up a chair to the desk as noisily as possible and slouched down into it. He looked at the captain and in a low tone said sarcastically, "My name is Edge.". "OK, smart-ass," said Eckersley as he rose from behind his desk, "Here is your reinstatement from IAD. They found the gun Ace pulled on you. One Doris Walker picked it up and put it in her purse. They busted her couple of days ago on a routine traffic stop. She admitted to picking it up," Eckersley continued his story. "Hate to have you back, but you are a good cop, so welcome back just the same." Eckersley looked at him and then down at the paperwork on his desk. Edge left the office to hugs and handshakes from the other detectives. "I am back," he said.

Foggy nights had been pretty frequent and unusual in Niagara Falls, especially that October. Some said it was the mist from the falls itself forming low-flying clouds around the city, but it could be atmospheric conditions causing the unusual phenomenon. Lake Erie was outside of Buffalo, which ran into the upper Niagara River, over the falls, into the lower Niagara River, and to Lake Ontario. This also could be a reason for late-season fog. The carriage sat at the old stone chimney near the closed Promex building. Inside the carriage were John and a streetwalker named Tiara Robinson. Tiara was a very attractive African-American woman—about five feet one, thin build, 114 pounds, and neatly dressed. She was very well known to frequent the center city area. John came across her at 11th and South Avenue as she was strolling her streets.

She was a woman who knew how to manipulate her tricks, and then steal everything they had or attempted to. Most of the time, she was looking to get high on anything. John stared into her soul through her dark-brown, sensual eyes, as if to hypnotize her in some sort of way. His gaze was mesmerizing, piercing into her, causing her to become flushed all over. She hadn't felt this way in a long time. She couldn't believe she was with a fine-looking specimen of a man such as this. "So what's we gonna do mister? I ain't gonna stare at you all night" she asked. "Do you see that chimney over there?" he asked, changing the subject. "It reminds me of home." "So what's that got to do with me?" she asked again. "It is a special area for me, and I thought you would like to be with me on this special night" "So, what's so special about tonight?" Tiara asked him. "We will get to that later, but right now I have something you might like, to make you relax a little" "What ya got? Coke? Crack? Weed?" she inquired. "Something better," he replied as he reached into his vest pocket and removed his snuff box. "Try this, it will help you relax." He opened the box, and she took a pinch and placed it in each nostril, sending the drug into her brain, causing instant convulsions. Her eyes became wide; her breathing labored as she tried to speak. Her body writhed violently, and then all was quiet. She was unconscious. John and his carriage driver carried Tiara and placed her in front of the chimney. The driver, Angus, left John alone with his unconscious friend, and John proceeded to do his work. John reached into his other vest pocket and removed a straight razor, slicing her clothing off first. He then sliced below the right ear across her throat to the left, sending arterial blood everywhere. He opened up her abdomen, exposing the viscera, and reached into the chest cavity to remove her heart. Grasping the heart, he held it into the air, whispering to himself "I have set you free, my black darling." John placed the heart into a wooden box, and then went into a frenzy, slicing everything on her body; her face was a bloody pulp when he was finished. He picked up the box and walked back to the carriage, smiling at what he had done.

Chapter Four

Niagara Falls was once a great and prosperous industrial city, with factories lining Buffalo Avenue, but high taxes from the state of New York and cheaper labor had sent the jobs to the southern states, as also the people with them. Some closed their doors due to overseas competition, eliminating many jobs. Corporate executives said it was not conducive to do business in New York if they didn't get cheap hydropower and tax breaks. Lt. Neil Woodredge stood at the railing of the American falls overlooking the Canadian side, with the Skylon Tower and the bright lights illuminating the night sky. He was reminiscing about the times when Niagara Falls was bustling with people. Old Falls Street was buzzing with people from all over the world. They came to see the mighty Niagara and its entire splendor—the roar of the water flowing swiftly over the brink. He could remember the Strand and Cataract theaters, the canal running through downtown, and thousands of people a year visiting this tourist attraction. Now urban renewal had set in, as well as the appearance of downtown with new hotels and the convention center. Times were changing. The Rapids theater was now gone, and much of Main street was boarded up. Everything was gone—Jenss was gone, and Slipkos Grocery was gone. It was a crying shame. Some said change was good and for the better, but on the other hand, was it? When he looked around the city, he saw the makings of a ghost town. Though some industries still remained, he thought of the city that once was and still could be a wonder of the world. Now everything was concentrating on tourism. The once proud Niagara Falls had a population of over one hundred thousand people, which had dwindled to just over fifty thousand people now. It didn't matter how many people there were, the drugs kept coming in. Buildings were burglarized; people were robbed and raped. Murders and vandalism didn't stop. Crime didn't take a day off. As Edge turned to leave the falls, heading back to his car, his cell phone rang, breaking his thought. "Hello," was the answer. "Edge, Eckersley here. I need you at the old stone chimney." "I'm on my way, skipper," Edge said. He thought to himself, "Never a dull moment around here. Never a dull moment."

Officer Steve Atkins was the first on the scene. He was a rookie cop at his first homicide scene, and it had to be the worst he had ever seen. Even anything on TV couldn't compare to this. He was on patrol when the tour bus operator waved him down and directed him to the gruesome sight. Edge arrived ten minutes later and approached Officer Atkins. "Hey Atkins, what ya got here?" he asked. "I hope you haven't eaten yet," Atkins said. It is a pretty horrible sight." Edge and Atkins walked to the chimney, and Edge peered at the dead woman. "That's fubar," Edge said. "Fubar?" asked Atkins as he looked at Edge with a strange expression. "Yea, fucked up beyond any recognition," Edge laughed as the rookie began to bring up his lunch. Captain Eckersley arrived and began to give orders to the fellow officers he had called in. The bus arrived to transport the body to the lab. CSI Charlie Mort and team began to gather evidence. The body was a lump of flesh, unrecognizable at that. They knew she was a black female, and that's all they had to go on. "Any witnesses?" Eckersley asked. "No," Edge said. "The tour bus operator found the body. We don't have much to go on, skipper," he continued. "What a sight for the tourists to see, huh Atkins," Edge said, laughing at him for losing his dinner all over the crime scene. "You know, lieutenant, you are a real prince," Atkins replied. "I know, officer, I know," Edge smirked at him.

Back at the lab, Charlie Mort began his examination with the help of the medical examiner. He removed the clothes and bagged them for forensics, then cleaned the body so the medical examiner could do the autopsy. The medical examiner was Robert James, a seasoned M.E. with a doctorate in forensic science. He began with the head, noticing all the slices on the face, especially the nose area. He took a swab of the nose area and then opened her mouth to swab for DNA. Charlie took them upstairs to the DNA technician. "We need an ID on the dead girl ASAP." he said. "I'll have it for you shortly," said the DNA tech. "I also need that swab I gave you with the blood on it analyzed—it seems to be compromised with a powdery substance. See what you can get for me on that. Thanks." "Will do," came the reply. Charlie returned to the morgue to continue his assistance as the medical examiner was checking her chest cavity. "Hey Charlie, she is heartless," Bob looked at him with a smirk. "Bad joke, Bob," Charlie said. "No, I mean she actually has no heart. Whoever killed her took the heart," he retorted. "What the hell is the killer going to do with the heart?" Charlie remarked. "Some killers take a trophy of some sort—in this case it's the heart," Bob added.

Edge entered the squad room and sat at his desk, when the phone rang. It was Charlie from the lab. "Hello Charlie," Edge said. "Come on, Edge, How did you know it was me calling?" Charlie asked. "The captain had interdepartmental caller ID installed in the system for better police communication," Edge told him. What do you have for me, Charlie?" Edge inquired. "Well, it seems she was drugged first, and then her throat was slit ear to ear. That would be the cause of death. The drug of choice for this murder was arsenic. There wasn't enough in her system to kill her, though. Arsenic in small amounts causes euphoria or unconsciousness. So it seems the murderer knocked her out with arsenic first, and then proceeded to butcher her." "Thanks for the info, Charlie. Bye" Edge hung up. Edge couldn't believe this day. What a day it was. Edge thought to himself, "I need a beer."

Chapter Five

Capt. Arthur Eckersley was meeting with Chief John Andersen concerning the recent homicide at the chimney. Captain Eckersley was in charge of the homicide bureau in Niagara Falls, but since murders were rare here, he was in charge of the detective bureau. Chief Andersen asked Eckersley, "Where do we stand on the murder at the chimney? Any leaks to the press outside of the normal statements?" "Well, Chief, the crime scene people are on top of the evidence they have collected. Lieutenant Woodredge is in charge of the case with Detective Cook. We have no witnesses at this point in time. What we do have is a dead female of African descent, badly mutilated beyond recognition. We are waiting on DNA results. The weapon used appears to be a sharp knife or surgical scalpel. Could be a straight razor too. She may be a streetwalker or homeless girl. Normal bullshit was given to the press, nothing of importance." "Keep me posted on any progress," Chief Andersen said. "Yes sir," said Eckersley as he left the chief's office.

Edge arrived at the morgue to see Charlie Mort. "Do we have an ID on the woman at the chimney?" he asked. "Yea, her name is Tiara Robinson, and she lives on South Avenue near Eleventh Street. She has a long rap sheet on her short life, mostly for prostitution and drugs." "Anything else I can use to keep the captain happy?" Edge asked. "The powdery substance in the nostrils mixed with the blood is arsenic," Charlie looked at him curiously. "Arsenic? That's interesting," Edge queried. "Why give her arsenic if you're going to slice her throat? Maybe to immobilize her so she won't fight back." Edge figured the killer was trying to relax them to prevent them from fighting him off. "Charlie, did you do a sex screen for semen anywhere?" Edge wondered. "Yes. It came back negative for semen. He didn't rape her or have sex with her," Charlie told him. "Thanks, Charlie, I'll be seeing ya." Edge left the morgue. After Edge left the morgue, he went to meet Abbie at the crime library, where she had been doing research on serial killers and macabre acts by individuals. When he arrived, she was studying Jack the Ripper on the internet. "Hey Abbie. What did you find?" he inquired. "There are a lot of sickos, weirdos, and perverts," she said. "Too many to count. I'm looking up Jack the Ripper right now." "Why him, sweetie," he asked as he looked at the screen. "Because he is the most interesting of them all, and he was never caught. He taunted Scotland

Yard to catch him, and they never did. He was a genius at this, you know, killing prostitutes and evading the police." she continued. "I'm trying to build a profile on this killer using similarities from other cases. Jack the Ripper comes close to this case. He butchered prostitutes." "I see where you are going with this. Smart—very smart," Edge smirked at her. "OK, smart ass, what's with the smirk?" she asked him. "You missed a good time at the morgue with Charlie," he said to her with a silly smile on his face, because he knew she would lose her stomach contents if she went. She can't stand the smell of the chemicals they use there. "You know Edge, you can be a total asshole all the time," Abbie looked at him sternly. "I know I can, but it's all in good taste and fun," he said to her. "Come on, let's get out of here and get a drink. We have been working long hours since I got off suspension. She turned to him and gave him a long, passionate kiss. They left and retired to his apartment for the evening.

Edge's problems stemmed since his rookie year, exactly to the day he was sworn in as a police officer. His smart-ass attitude began the day he entered the academy, almost getting him tossed from the program. He had the answers to all the questions, usually derogatory in nature and sarcastic as they come. His instructors were more than irritated, and they tried to berate him in front of his fellow classmates, only to have him turn the tables on them. His unorthodox ways and streetwise values seemed to anger the police instructors even more. During defensive tactics, they tried to disable him more than once, only to have him take charge and embarrass the hell out of them. Every chance they could get, it was an opportunity for the instructor to try to flunk him out. But he was far too intelligent for any of them. He would pull many practical jokes and belittle all of them. They knew who it was but couldn't prove anything. One time, during a front choke hold demonstration, the instructor whose name was Leon Adams—a huge African-American with twenty-five-inch biceps—grabbed his throat with both hands, a little too tight for Edge's taste. Edge grabbed both of his pinky fingers and spread them apart, snapping both. All he could do was hang his hands limp at his sides and writhe in pain, giving Edge much respect after that. Edge didn't have any problems with any of the instructors after that. They knew he wasn't playing any games. He finished at the top of his class in defensive tactics and was asked to join the team. He politely declined, since teaching wannabees wasn't his gig. From then on his reputation was intact, and everyone in the department would him give him the respect he deserved—even Captain (Clown) Eckersley.

Chapter Six

The end of October, the weather started getting colder and fall started to settle in, with the leaves changing color and falling from the trees. It brought much color to the area. It was a tranquil time of year with the summer tourist season ending and winter tourist season beginning—a different kind of tourist coming in, one who begins with murder. This year was different as Edge lay on his bed with Abbie next to him. He was contemplating the case in his head. Unable to sleep, he got up from the bed and opened the French doors to let the cool night air in. He lit a smoke and stared onto Third Street into the night. So far, it was a quiet night. He turned and looked at Abbie as she slept, glad to have her back. Edge finished the cigarette and flicked the butt out onto Third Street. He went back to bed and drifted off to sleep.

October 31, Halloween, when all the beggars start trick-or-treating. Maybe the killer would come out tonight. Edge awoke to the ringing of his cell phone. Eckersley was on his caller ID. "Hello Captain," Edge said wearily, "What's going on this early in the morning?" "I need you and Cook at 18th and South stat. We have another body. Tell her to hurry up and get her clothes on," said Eckersley as Edge hung up the phone, not to hear him laughing. He got Abbie up; they quickly showered and dressed, then headed to 18th and South.

As Edge and Abbie arrived at the location, Captain Eckersley had taken charge of the crime scene. "What do we have here?" Edge asked him as Abbie looked on. "We have a Caucasian female, young, butchered beyond recognition. The neighbor found her about half hour ago," the captain continued in between shouting orders. Edge walked over to the body, knelt down, and noticed empty eye sockets. "Why did he take her eyes?" a notable question with the answer coming soon—maybe too soon. Maybe he was building a body like Dr. Frankenstein or something of that nature. There were so many variables to consider. There were so many questions he needed answers for as he was caught in thought "We definitely have a serial killer on our hands," Abbie and the captain agreed. "Now the question is, how do we catch him?" the captain asked. "With a decoy," Edge cut in. "We set up a decoy streetwalker, audio—wired and surrounded by undercover officers. We catch him in the act, but nobody gets hurt." "But who is going to be the decoy," asked Abbie as the captain and Edge looked at her smiling.

Edge walked over to where Charlie was standing and asked him if there was anything new about this murder versus the last. Charlie nodded that there were similarities except the missing organs. “They were both pretty mangled up, Edge. The only difference is, this girl is missing her eyes.” “No shit, Charlie,” Edge hammered back at him. “Your powers of observation simply amaze me at times.” “Well, Edge, I have to get back to the morgue to get busy on this one. See ya later.” “One more thing, Charlie, did she have arsenic in her nostrils?” Edge asked. “It appears that way, Edge, but I’ll send you a complete report when I finish with the examination.” Edge nodded and looked away. He thought to himself, it’s time to catch a killer—time to teach this murderer a lesson. Edge stood there, looking around the area, thinking about the frustration certain cases will provide. The bus left with the body and the area was secured. Captain Eckersley had left a few minutes earlier. Edge looked at Abbie, and she noticed a worried look in his eyes. She touched his face lightly and said “Don’t worry about me being the decoy. I’ll be all right, ’cause you will be there to protect me. I’m in good hands, you know,” as she kissed him lightly on the lips, smiling at him. “Come on, let’s get out of here.”

Chapter Seven

After a night at the casino, losing a ton of dough and having too much to drink,Tammie Martin was on her way home. She decided on Second Street as her path to her destination. Behind the Bank of America, she stopped at the ATM to draw out a little cab cash, as it was beginning to rain. As she was leaving the bank, she noticed off in the shadows a man—tall, dressed in black—standing there looking at her. She opened her cell phone and called a taxi to the bank. Tammie proceeded to the front of the bank near the side parking area and waited. She was hoping it would hurry, since the man in the shadows was approaching, and she was fearful he might be some sort of weirdo. As he came up to her, he tipped his hat and gave her a bidding of good evening. She just looked at him, not answering his bidding. It was getting foggy out, and she was apprehensive about her situation. He faced her now and asked her, "Are you in distress, madam? Do you need to be taken anywhere?" She looked up into his eyes—his strange, dark amber eyes; they were hypnotically in a sense of being in a trance as she let herself be seduced by them. Her reply was, "Yes, mister, I do need a ride." He guided her to the carriage. She wasn't sure if the alcohol was causing her to lose her ability of reason or she was mesmerized by his gentlemanly demeanor. Maybe a little of both. As she climbed into the carriage, he following her in, she noticed how clean and gorgeous it was inside, with red velvet cushions and a partial bar, with what appeared to be brandy snifters and a bottle of brandy secured to the shelf. She looked at his face, with a nice handlebar mustache and goatee. His hair was partially long, just over his ears, and from what she could tell, combed neatly as he kept his carriage. He tapped the roof with his cane, and the driver started the carriage moving, or it appeared so. He greeted her again, "I bid you a good evening. Are you more at ease now?" "Yes," was the reply. "Where can my carriage take you?" he asked. "I'd like to be taken to Ferry and Portage, please." she said politely. "My name is John," he told her. "And yours, my dear lady?" "Tammie. My name is Tammie Martin," was her reply. "A beautiful name for you," said he as he bent to kiss her hand, which she thought was unusual, but just as nice, since no one ever did that before. "A perfect gentleman," she thought. John reached for his snuff box and took a tiny pinch up each nostril, inhaling strongly, to get the full effect of the drug. "Care for a snort of snuff?" he asked her graciously. She reached for the snuff, and after snorting some in both nostrils, she felt strange and warm all over. Tammie sat there for a moment as the drug ascended into her brain, causing her endorphins to go spastic. Her body started convulsing, she began banging her head against the carriage side, and finally she lay still, unconscious. John and Angus carried Tammie to the side of the parking area off of Second Street.

John began his macabre butchery the same as before, by slicing her from ear to ear across the throat. He sliced her breasts and proceeded to her abdomen, where he sliced her just above the naval around the sides, and then opened the flap, exposing her organs. He then removed her stomach and placed it in a wooden box. He finished by slicing her face unrecognizable as he had previously done.

Behind the amphitheater building, Leonard was finishing a Silver Thunder forty-ouncer when he saw the carriage coming out of fog. He looked at the bottle and then back at the carriage and horses. After the carriage left, Leonard staggered over to the spot where John had mutilated his prey. Through his drunken stupor, he looked down at the most horrific scene he had ever witnessed. Her clothes were in disarray and she was mangled beyond recognition. He stood there a moment, thinking about what to do. Leonard began to run, until he was far away from the area, where his forty was forcing its way up. "I'm never going to drink again," he thought.

November 2, the parking attendant discovered Tammie's body. He dialed 911 and told the dispatcher to which side of the parking area to meet him. He looked down at her again, astonished at the bloody scene. Officer Aaron Brown was first to arrive and secure the scene, trying not to contaminate anything. Lieutenant Woodredge and Detective Cook arrived shortly after that. Edge bent down to the body and studied it intensely. He looked up at Abbie and said, "Same M.O. as the other two." Abbie couldn't believe what her eyes were seeing. The mutilation was unbelievable. Her stomach started to feel uneasy and she walked away with tears in her eyes. Edge noticed she was upset and walked over to comfort her. "Abbie, this is what we signed up for when we decided to become police officers," he explained to her. "I know it, Edge, but this is too much—her organs and everything is hanging out. This guy is a sick individual." "That's why we have to get him, and I need your help, sweetheart," he said as he hugged her. "I need you to be strong," he added. "OK, Edge, give me a minute to gather myself. I'm sorry, I just never encountered anything this gruesome before. Dead bodies I can deal with, this was little much. I'll be all right in a second," she said as he walked over to resume his examination. The coroner and CSI team arrived to gather the evidence. Charlie looked at Edge and said, "Same as the others." "Yea, Charlie, same M.O.," Edge replied, "Get me an ID and keep me posted on anything else." Edge started walking away, and Charlie said, "I'll give you an ID right now. Her name is Tammie Martin and address is 1425 Ferry Ave. All her money is accounted for and credit cards are all here. So robbery is out of the question. She has the powdery substance in her nostrils, so she has been snorting tonight. Also it appears that her stomach is missing." "Thanks, Charlie," said Edge as he walked to where the captain and Abbie were standing. "We have to get this guy before he gets all the organs he needs. The stomach is missing from this one," He informed. The captain looked at Edge and said, "Trophies. Every murderer takes a trophy. This one's no different." Edge looked at both the captain and Abbie, "Let's get Operation Decoy going, so we can nail this one once and for all."

Edge had seen Abbie around the department since she joined the force some years earlier, and continued to keep his eye on her every chance he had. Wherever Detective Abigail Cook went, Edge seemed to be there. He even followed her into the women's room to talk to her, but couldn't get the nerve, so he would sneak out and wait by the door. She would give him the woman's look—you know, the look that says leave it well enough alone. Edge couldn't do that, since his infatuation was just too strong. He would make her his girl even if it cost him his job. There were many times she would go to her captain and tell him that Edge was stalking her. The captain would tell her to forget it because he was harmless, except to criminals. He told her Edge was a good cop and that she would some day be glad he was around. When she made the detective grade, Edge asked Captain Eckersley if he could partner with her and show her the ropes as a detective. The rest was history.

Chapter Eight

Niagara Gazette reporter Andrew Blair arrived at his desk at 9:00 a.m. on November 5, to a parcel with no return address, wrapped in plain brown paper. "Did anyone see who delivered this package?" he asked throughout the room. "It was sitting outside of the building," came the reply from a fellow reporter. With all the terrorism going on in the world, he was beginning to wonder about this package. He thought to himself, why anyone would want to bomb or destroy the Gazette; they would want the press to recognize their work. He shrugged it off and decided to open it anyway. He slowly opened the brown wrapping to discover a cigar box with the writing "London Cigar Company" written on the top. Andy lifted the clasp, opened the lid, and was astounded at what he saw inside. A pair of eyes staring back at him. "Holy shit!" he said, "Dial 911." Everyone crowded around the desk to see what Andy was cursing at. They all stared—some walked away in disbelief, while others oohed and aahed and talked among themselves.

Lieutenant Woodredge and Detective Cook arrived and walked into the reporters' room to a very upset Andy. Edge had known Andy from the story he wrote about the shooting of Ace. Andy was a good reporter and only printed the facts—not this garbage you get in the tabloids. Edge respected him for that. The two detectives peered into the box and noticed the eyes. "Now we are getting somewhere, Abbie. He just made contact," Edge said, "We will take this to the lab, Andy." As he began to pick up the box, Abbie stopped him. "What's that on the lid? It's a piece of paper with words on it—it reads 'The eyes of the law'," read Abbie. "Good eyes, Abbie—very good eyes," he looked at her and smiled. "You're a sick puppy, Edge. Very bad pun, if you ask me," Abbie retorted, but couldn't help but smirk as they left with the box. She didn't want to say anything up in reporters' room about the signature. It was written in French script as follows:

The eyes of the law signed J.

Abbie and Edge sat in the car looking at the paper. "He gave us the initial of his first name, that's a plus for us," Abbie said. "That was a good find on your part and a good idea not to expose it to the press," Edge told her. They were both excited about this lead and went directly to Captain Eckersley to keep him informed. The captain looked into the box and then told them to get it directly to the lab to Charlie. When they arrived at the lab, Charlie already knew what they were bringing him. "I know what you have, Edge. Andy called and told me, and I know whose eyes they are. Her name is Jillian, because I found a necklace around her neck amidst the blood with that name on it. I need to connect it to a last name. Maybe one of her hooker friends might report her as missing." "So much for surprises, huh, Charlie," Edge smiled at him. "They are gorgeous eyes, though. They follow you around the room like the Mona Lisa," and Edge chuckled. "Come on, asshole, let's go before you become unbearable to be with," Abbie said, pulling him along. "Let's get this going. We have to meet the captain tonight. You are a real dick brain, Edge," she said.

Detective Abigail Cook knew what kind of a man Edge was since first meeting him, or should I say, seeing him when she first joined the force. He was a pain in the ass—a straightforward, no-nonsense cop who didn't take any shit from anyone, especially from authority. He was a sarcastic bastard, and his sense of humor left little to be desired. He was strange in a weird sort of way, but his dedication to his job went without merit. She had learned much from him since joining the detective squad and knew he would have her back if anything were to happen. She was glad he recommended her for his partnership in more ways than one. They had to be mum on that part of their personal life since Captain Eckersley was not fond of partners who slept together. He said it was against department policy, but it seemed no other captains enforced it but him. To save face they decided to keep that part of their relationship out of the office. She got used to his quick quips and sarcastic comments. His belligerent attitude only seemed to strengthen their hold on each other, and she knew when to leave him in thought in his own world. He would go off by himself and think things through. Upon returning, he would be in a better frame of mind—usually horny. He would tell her that all the thinking would give him a woodie. She being the good woman she was, would take care of that problem promptly. She remembered their first love session on top of the car on the service road at the old power plant. It was a dandy. She was in never-never land when she made love to him. She knew he loved her even though he never said it, because that was his way. She had told him many times that she loved him, but his only response was the usual puppy dog look he would give her, and she knew her answer. Sometimes he was overprotective, and she had to remind him that she could take care of herself. Sometimes he would give in, and then again, maybe not. There wasn't any way anyone could disrespect her and not feel his wrath—whether verbal or physical. He was strong and good-looking. He could probably get any woman he wanted, if she could put up with his attitude. Abbie would put him in his place if he got too bold. All in all, she loved every inch of him (chuckle).

Chapter Nine

In the office of Captain Eckersley were present Edge; detectives Cook, Reyes, and Olivio; and of course the captain. The skipper started the briefing by saying that Detective Cook's safety was of utmost priority. "This is the way this operation is going to unfold. Cook's the decoy. Edge, Olivio, and Reyes are the backup officers. I want her in sight at all times. Cook will wire up. We have no witnesses to the murders. Let's stay on our toes on this one. This might be our only chance at getting this guy." "May I say something, Captain?" asked Cook. "Sure Cook, let's hear your thoughts." "I have been doing some research on arsenic, and in the nineteenth century it was used as a drug to get high on. It was the drug of choice back then." "I believe Charlie already deduced that in the lab," said Eckersley. "Let's not let it get to that. Be ready at 1:00 a.m. Do you have a location picked out, lieutenant?" he asked. "I was thinking of the Nineteenth Street and Niagara Street area," Said Edge. "That sounds good to me," the captain responded, "Any objections?" No one made a sound, and Operation Decoy was about to commence. "Everyone will be in constant communication. Got it people?" Everyone agreed.

At 1:00 a.m. everyone met the captain at Niagara Street. "Edge, you will be at MacKenna Avenue, Olivio is at Cudaback, and Reyes at Falls Street. I'll be at Niagara Street. All right, let's get into position," Eckersley commanded. Detective Cook started her strut down Nineteenth Street toward Falls Street, and everyone sounded off that they were in position. All kept her in sight as they waited for the night stalker. Abbie hit Cudaback when Leonard came out of nowhere, startling her a little. "You shouldn't be out here, you know. I have seen what he can do, you know. It is terrible, I mean, horrible. I saw him and his horse and buggy." stated Leonard. Leonard turned and ran. "Did everyone get that?" she asked. "10-4" came all replies. "We will get Leonard later," the captain said. At around 2:30 a.m., a fog started to come through from the falls area and was getting thicker fast. "Hey Captain, anything about a fog tonight in the forecast?" asked Edge. "Negative, Edge. I don't like it. Let's abort the operation," the captain said. "Let's move in now," was the command. "Abbie, you there?" Edge asked. "Come on, Detective Cook, respond now," the captain said. "Abbie, Abbie, come in. Do you hear me? It's Edge. Come on, Abbie." Abbie couldn't hear anything but static. Everyone closed in on Edge's location, but there was no sign of Detective Cook. "Where did she go?" asked Edge. "She has to be around here somewhere. Nobody saw her?" he asked, to a shaking of heads. Everyone was stumped as to where she had gone. "I want every available unit here, to search the area. We are not leaving until she is located," Edge commanded.

The carriage seemed to be slowly moving through the streets, but in reality it was at a standstill in an alley off of MacKenna Avenue. Abbie couldn't see a thing through the fog. Across from her was John, staring at her beauty and lovely cinnamon hair. "Who are you? And where am I?" Abbie demanded to know. "My carriage," was his reply. "How did I get in here?" again she demanded. "You stepped in of your own accord," again he replied. "Of course, I invited you in," he told her. "It seems you are a different kind of woman," he said. He looked into her eyes, hypnotizing her with his stare, trying to see into her soul, but she broke the gaze, drew her service weapon, and pointed at him, to his surprise. Astonishment was the look on his face. "Who are you?" she asked him sternly. "My dear lady, you will not need that firearm. My name is John, and I mean you no harm. And you are?" he asked her. "Detective Abigail Cook, Niagara Falls Police," she responded. "What do you want with me?" she asked. "Just your pleasant company," John said. 'You will not shoot me with that, so put it away. It will change the course of history if you do. Besides, I haven't done anything wrong." "Change history, what do you mean?" "Well, like I said, my name is John, but most people know me as Jack. I hail from London, England. Now do you know me?" he asked. "You are Jack the Ripper," she said. "Maybe I should just shoot you dead and save Scotland Yard a lot of problems trying to catch you, and maybe save some women's lives in England." "You could, but that wouldn't stop me from the task I have already done. My job is already finished there," he replied. "I like your city, Detective. It has a waterfall and a deep gorge, with beautiful lakes and rivers." "How did you get here?" Abbie asked him. "Now that's the puzzling question. I was in a rainstorm with thunder and lightning, and the next thing I know, I'm here, he told her. "We can discuss that further at a later date. See you later, Detective," said he as Abbie lay unconscious in the MacKenna Avenue alley.

Edge was the first to hear her moan and ran over to her, picking her up in his arms. He slightly tapped her face, asking her if she was all right. Her eyes opened slightly, and Edge was relieved that she seemed OK. The other detectives and the captain also came over to check her status. Abbie was groggy, but OK. Edge carried her to the car and set her in it. She began to stir, and he shook her slightly until she was semiconscious. "Abbie, its Edge. Are you all right? As she was beginning to arouse, she was whispering something; it sounded like Jack. "It's Jack, she said and then drifted off again. "Take her to the hospital and get her checked out," the captain said to Edge. Edge arrived at the emergency entrance and hospital personnel were quickly out. They placed Abbie on a gurney and wheeled her into a treatment room. "What happened to her?" the resident doctor asked. "I don't exactly know. Check her for arsenic," Edge replied, "She may have been drugged." After hours in emergency, Edge finally got word that she was all right. Slightly delirious from the arsenic, she was going to be just fine. "We want to keep an eye on her overnight for observation," the doctor told Edge. "OK, can I see her?" asked Edge. "Just for a minute," the doctor replied. She has had quite an ordeal. Edge walked into Abbie's room, "Hey babe, how are you doing?" he asked, "You look better than when I found you." "I feel weak, is all, Edge," she responded. "He gave you a dose of arsenic. You are lucky it wasn't lethal," Edge told her, "Hey, you get some rest and we will talk later. Take care, Abbie." "You too, Edge. Bye" she said as she drifted off to sleep.

Edge knew he didn't have her back and had guilty feelings about it. If only he had moved in sooner, she might not be in this state. He had to get this dirtbag even if it was the last thing he did as a cop. He couldn't care less what happened to him, but Abbie was his life. He wasn't fond of her being the decoy, but they both knew the risks as police officers when they signed on. He continued to second guess his decision, but to no avail. He couldn't shake off the guilt. He needed a beer.

Chapter Ten

Edge left the hospital feeling a bit guilty that Abbie was exposed to this killing animal. Why he didn't kill her left him mystified. Maybe he knew that she wasn't a lady of the evening. All the questions would soon be answered when Abbie got out of the hospital. Now he had to face the captain with explanations as to what went wrong. He felt in his own mind, nothing did go wrong. Everyone was in position and on alert. Even the captain was there to supervise. As Edge continued to cogitate on the thought, something was bothering him about the whole scenario. It was the fog. The fog was so thick you could slice it with a knife, no pun intended. You couldn't see your hand in front of your face. The killer knew that, and it was his cover. It seemed the killer had been at this awhile. He did his dirty deed under the cover of the fog. But fog was unusual this time of year, unless he brings the fog with him. Thoughts ran through his mind, and questions kept nagging at him. Finally he concluded that he would not put Abbie in that position again. Edge arrived at his apartment on Third Street, went to the fridge for a cold brew, and stood outside on his balcony. He sipped his beer and lit a cigarette as he was looking along Third Street, the traffic moving along slowly. His thoughts were on Abbie and how much he cared for her—how much they shared with each other and how he almost lost her. He finished his ciggy and flicked it out on Third Street. He finished his beer and collapsed on the bed, where sleep overtook him.

When Edge awoke, it was 4:00 p.m. He took a shower and dressed; all the while his thoughts were on Abbie. He got into his car and was off to the hospital to check on her. Arriving at her room, he noticed she was still asleep. He left for the station. Edge walked into the station and right into Captain Eckersley's office. "Good afternoon, lieutenant," Eckersley said. Edge, in turn, had the same reply. "Abbie's still asleep, skipper," Edge said to him. "Yes, I know, Edge. I have been in communication with the hospital and been getting updates on her condition." the captain told him. "Did Detective Cook say anything to you when you found her?" "Yea, she mentioned the name Jack a couple of times," he relayed the information. "What it means is anyone's guess. When Abbie wakes, I'll go and talk to her." "So, where do you think this guy will strike next?" Captain Eckersley asked. "In my opinion, he will strike wherever the hookers are walking the streets. We have to get the hookers off the streets. Even if it means arresting the lot of them, to protect them. Once they get the word that we are out there getting them off the street, they will probably go underground and hide," Edge continued. "We won't get them all, lieutenant," stated the captain. "We can't hold them that long." "Well, what do you suggest, Captain?" Edge asked. "The only thing is to keep an eye on them and see what develops," the captain stated. "I'll get the RAC patrol out there and see if they can stir things up with these ladies." "OK skipper, I'll see you later."

The RAC patrol was short for Roving Anti Crime in Niagara Falls and was effective in solving street crimes. They dressed in plain clothes, not looking like your ordinary police officers. They were effective in drug deals and the ladies of the evening. They traveled in unmarked cars and looked like the everyday person on the street. Edge used to be one of them until he went to homicide. So, they knew each other well and were well liked by everyone, even the criminals. Sgt. Dashawn Johnson was in charge of the RAC patrol. He was a big man, standing six foot five and weighing about 260 pounds of solid muscle. He had five other undercover men and one female under his command. He knew of the killings of the hookers and kept his crew on the lookout for this murderer. He was meeting with his people when Captain Eckersley came in and announced top priority on these homicides. "I need every available body on these killings," the captain said. "Do I make myself clear, people? Sergeant, is that understood?" Eckersley commanded. "Yes, sir," the sergeant hammered back. "OK guys and gal, let's get our eyes and ears out there and find a killer," the sergeant announced. The meeting was adjourned and everyone went to their cars and hit the street. Anything suspicious was their objective.

Edge was at the hospital sitting with Abbie at her bedside chair, watching her stir as if she was engaged with this character. She was pretty restless, probably reenacting her ordeal. Edge whispered to her, trying to awaken her, but to no avail; she was out of it. The nurse heard him and came in. "Lieutenant, now you were told to leave her to rest. If you're not going to comply with hospital rules, I will have to ask you to leave." "Yes ma'am," came Edge's reply. "I'll be a good boy." "Very well," the nurse said with a stern expression on her face. Edge left the room and went to the gift shop downstairs in the lobby. Upon his return, Abbie was awake, and he presented her with a bouquet of flowers. She looked up at him smiling to her as he gave her the flowers. "How are you, Edge?" she asked. "No, I think the question is how you are Abbie?" he returned the question with a question. "Oh, I've been better," she replied. "What happened to me?" she asked him. "It seems he gave you a dose of arsenic, and you have been out for a while. But you're going to be all right. Thank God for that." "Since when are you into thanking God?" she smiled at him. He smiled back and bent to give her a kiss on the cheek. "Hey, look babe, we'll talk when you feel up to it. OK?" "OK, Edge. Thanks for the flowers," she said as she closed her eyes and drifted off to sleep. Edge knew she needed rest, and he left her to head back to the station to go over the case files again and to check on what Abbie was working on. All the research she was doing could maybe give him a clue as to who Jack was. It was 8:30 p.m. when he arrived, went over to Abbie's desk, and picked up a file labeled "Jack the Ripper." He took it over to his desk, sat down, and began reading the case file on Jack the Ripper—the scourge of London in the nineteenth century. As he read, he noticed many similarities between the case investigated by Scotland Yard and the case he was involved in. Even if it was Jack the Ripper, he would have to be dead by now. His thoughts were now composed of both cases and how similar they were, and he thought to himself maybe there was a copycat killer who worshipped The Ripper. The Ripper would tease the police with body parts and letters, tempting them to catch him. Unfortunately they were unable too. Back in the eighteen hundreds, forensics was just beginning to surface. Besides that, The Ripper left no clues for them to work with—no fingerprints or anything whatsoever. We have the same problem, and this is the twenty-first century. Whoever he is, is very smart, quick, and knowledgeable with a blade, and he knows his way around the body anatomy-wise. Edge compared the crime scene photos of both cases and the bodies were basically the same—young women brutally butchered and body parts removed. The difference was the locations. He sat there examining the cases, and the longer he looked, he was resolved that he was dealing with a ripper-type character, whether it be the original Jack the Ripper or a copycat. After all, Abbie did mention the name Jack. His concentration was broken by Detective Reyes with an envelope in his hand. "Hey Edge, this came for Abbie today," Reyes said. "Who delivered it?" Edge asked. "It came via mail—no return address," Reyes told him. The envelope was tan in color and addressed to Abbie in old-world script. Edge carefully picked it up and carried it to the forensic lab. He knew there would be no fingerprints on it, but just in case, he would have Charlie check it out. "Hey Charlie, will you dust this for prints for me?" Edge handed it to Charlie, and he began his work. "Mind if I open it and dust the inside?" Charlie asked him. "By all means, dust everything on it," Edge looked at him sternly. Charlie finished his dusting and turned to Edge and said "Nada, nothing, not even a partial." "Thanks, Charlie," said Edge as he took the letter back to his desk and began reading it. There was no date on it, and it was definitely strange handwriting—nothing you would see this day and age. It began:

Dear Abbie,

I am sorry our visit was brief as I was called away.

I hope to meet with you again as I find you an interesting Inspector

In your profession. I, myself are an interesting also in my
Profession but I don't feel our paths will cross anytime soon. I
Love your fair city and its choice of female companions. Your
Auburn hair and your attractiveness appeals to me greatly. I
Would have loved to get to know you better if we had more time.
If you have a male companion, I would assume he would be in
The same profession. This is unbecoming me. We are both
Opposites. I will be in your city again on the next lightning.
Until then I bid you a farewell.

Sincerely,
John

As Edge read the letter, he had a feeling of jealously. How dare this idiot try to come on to my woman? He knew this was an obsession—a purposeful, strong obsession, in which he knew that Abbie was still in danger. This nutcase might just come after her again. We have to get the proof or catch him in the act of his hideous crime. He must show this letter to the captain to keep him informed. If he didn't, he would not hear the end of his peril. The captain would chastise him until no end.

Chapter Eleven

As Detective Abigail Cook lay in the hospital bed staring at the ceiling, a plain white one at that, she thought about what had happened to her, trying to remember the events that took place, but drawing blanks on everything except the name Jack. Which Jack was she thinking about? She looked about the room as if the answers would run down the white walls to the blue part and then walk along the floor and smack her in the face, but not one answer would beseech her. As she stared out the window—her view of Tenth Street—she could see the cars passing along as people went about their daily routine—people entering the hospital and people leaving, going about their business as usual. She began to ponder what Edge was doing and how she could help him from her hospital room. She was even getting bored with the TV as the judge shows were beginning with the people's court. Sometimes she burst out laughing at some of the defendants and their excuses for not paying their bills. Sometimes Abbie thought these shows were half comedy and half legal procedures. She lay there, half wondering if the people really paid the judgment or a fund was set up by the sponsors for appearing on the show. She continued to watch as the judge humiliated the defendant, or sometimes the plaintiff—whichever got cockier. Her eyes seemed to drift off to dreamland as her subconscious mind took over revealing the details of her ordeal. She could recall, subconsciously of course, the beginning when she stepped into John's carriage the red velvet interior and the blackness of her surrounding area. Across from her sat John, with his eyes staring into her soul, hypnotizing with the power of evil. She could recall how she took the arsenic voluntarily and blacked out, but not after a short conversation with the man across from her. She was beginning to remember the conversation vividly, and that she had her weapon pointed at him, unable to pull the trigger. It was something he said about changing the course of history. What did he mean by that? She could remember his words as being said to her—"You will not shoot me because you will change the course of history, and you do not want to do that." His voice was calm and his demeanor mild as he spoke. His English accent was eloquent and his actions that of a gentleman. He was an educated man. He dressed all in black except for his shirt which was white, and his cape was black with a red inner lining. He wore a top hat like the one Lincoln had worn during the

Civil War. He appeared to be a very distinguished-looking man. He drank a fine sherry as he sat there looking at her, offering a glass which she sternly declined. When she awoke in the alley to Edge asking her if she was all right, all she could think of was Jack. Thinking about the last thing he said, "They call me Jack,' Abbie woke suddenly and sat up in bed with beads of sweat on her forehead. She needed to contact Edge at once to tell him everything she had dreamed of and to call Scotland Yard at once to ask for files of Jack the Ripper. She knew it had to be him. The brutality of the murders and the removal of organs—it just stands to reason. She also thought it was a copycat killer who worshipped the ripper, but that was highly unlikely. Abbie pressed the button for the nurse—a brightly dressed brunette with a pretty face and slender body—who arrived momentarily and asked her if she needed help with something? Abbie replied to her, "I need a phone, and quickly. I need to call Lt. Neil Woodredge at the police headquarters. I need to talk to him immediately. It's very important," as her voice sounded almost hysterical with emotion and panic. "OK," the nurse told her, "I will call the lieutenant for you and see if he will come up and see you." "Thank you, nurse," Abbie said calmly.

Edge was sitting at Abbie's desk speaking to Detective Reyes about what went on that night—about the fog coming in and then Abbie disappearing without any warning or communication between them. They came to the conclusion that Abbie was unable to transmit because of some kind of electrical interference. As Detective Reyes was about to speak, the phone interrupted him. He pick the receiver up and said, "Detective Reyes, Homicide, speaking. May I help you?" "Yes, this is the nurse at the hospital. I need to speak to a Detective Woodredge please, concerning Abigail Cook." Reyes handed the phone to Edge and said, "It's the nurse at the hospital." Edge grabbed the phone and said, "This is Lieutenant Woodredge. Can I help you, nurse?" "Yes, Abigail Cook has been asking for you. She sounds frantic about something. She said get here as soon as you can." "OK, I'm on the way." "What the hell is going on?" asked Reyes. "Abbie is fully awake, frantic about something and asking to see me. Do you want to go with me?" Reyes grabbed his coat before Edge could finish because he wanted to find out also if she was all right.

Chapter Twelve

Edge and Reyes ran past everyone in the room and past the captain's office with strange looks following them from the other detectives there. They got into the elevator and went to the basement where the unmarked cars are kept. They found their car, put the key into ignition, and heard the roar of the engine. Edge squealed the tires out of the underground garage and up the ramp onto Ferry Avenue to Hyde Park Boulevard. Edge turned on his police lights to pass through the red light onto Walnut Avenue. That's the good part of the job of a policeman—you can turn your lights on and pass traffic signals and signs. He red-lighted all the way to the hospital and parked on Tenth Street. Edge and Reyes left the car on Tenth Street and entered the hospital to the security guard's desk, where the guard told them they couldn't park there because it was for patient pick-up and drop-off only. They both showed him their badges simultaneously as they entered the elevator, pressing the third-floor button. It seemed like forever before the elevator reached the third floor. Once the doors opened, they quickly entered room 350, and Abbie was lying there, completely calm. Edge went to the nurse's station and asked what was going on with his partner. The nurse explained to him that she was beginning to get out of control and they had to sedate her. "Did she say anything?" he asked. "About what?" the nurse replied. "About anything. What are you, fucking stupid? Look it's important as to what she said before you knocked her out. It has to do with the case we were working on before she was put in here." "That's patient confidentiality," the nurse came back with a stern look on her face. "Look it here, nurse bitch, if another woman gets killed because you are withholding pertinent information, I will personally put the handcuffs on you myself and charge you with being an accomplice to murder. Now what did she say?" he looked at her with his own stern look. "All right," the nurse said, "but I better not lose my job over this. She kept saying Jack the Ripper over and over again. She was talking crazy. She kept saying she needed to talk to you immediately and that Jack the Ripper was stalking Niagara Falls. That she had met and spoken to him in his carriage. I thought it was the valium we gave her causing her to hallucinate. That's all she said." "When she wakes, call me at once," Edge commanded, "or it will be your job," as Reyes looked on but said nothing. Edge and Reyes walked away to the elevators. Reyes turned to Edge and said to him "Don't you think you were a little hard on her?" "Hard my ass. We have a killer out there taking out women and you think I'm being a hard ass. She is lucky I acted more civil than I usually am. If she was a dude, she would have been in cuffs on her way to jail for obstruction." They both entered the elevator and arrived at the entrance a moment later. "Where are we going now?" asked Reyes. "To teach the hookers the good word," replied Edge. "What's the good word?" Reyes asked. Edge looked at Reyes and said in a smooth tone, "Get the fuck off the street or die!" Reyes snickered and looked out his window, shaking his head because he knew Edge wasn't joking when it came to doing his job, but his manners of speaking leaved little to be desired. At the intersection of Nineteenth Street and Niagara Street, they noticed Tina hanging around the corner in front of the laundromat, dressed in a nice short skirt and black stockings with a cheap ass-fur coat—a cheap knockoff if Edge ever saw one. They rolled up on her and she turned to walk away down Nineteenth Street. Edge turned the corner off of Niagara Street in the same direction as Tina. The car was adjacent to her and Reyes rolled down the window. Tina approached the car and looked at Edge with an "Oh shit, not you again" expression. She looked at them both and asked, "Why you hasslin' me? I ain't doing nothing but hanging with the homies." "I got a message for you, Tina, and you better get it right the first and spread the good word. Get the fuck off the streets or die! Ya got it, Tina? Spread the good word around to all the other scum-sucking ladies of the evening. If you don't get the good word, I will arrest you and place you in protective custody for your good." "Gotcha Edge, I'm outta here," Tina smiled at him. "I will come and live at your crib. That way I will get complete protection." "Not this time, baby. I already have a roommate, and I don't think she would appreciate it if you stayed even one night," Edge explained to her. "Don't do me like this, Edge. How about you, Reyes?" she looked at Reyes with his shit-eating grin on his face, and he looked at Edge, then back at her, and replied "Naw, I don't want to walk out with any friends I didn't walk in with." "Fuck you both and the pigs you rode in on." She looked at them laughing. "Watch your back, Tina" Edge told her as they drove away to find as many as they could before the ripper did.

Captain Eckersley called Edge on his cell and told him he needed to see him at the station as soon as possible. Edge and Reyes arrived twenty minutes later and met at the CO's office. The captain acknowledged them and they sat down, both looking and waiting for the captain to speak. He looked at both of them and said "Where were you guys going in such a hurry?" "We had to get to the hospital because Abbie was going spastic and the nurse called me to let me know she was awake and wanted to see me right away. By the time we arrived there they had placed her under sedation again. So we were unable to talk to her. She was out of it totally," Edge explained to him. Again he looked at them and said "Let's go over the evidence and see what we have to go on," the captain said. "Well," Edge said, "We have three dead hookers with much fubar, and we have arsenic as his mode of immobilization before he does his butchery. Also we have organs from the victims that were sent to the local paper. We know he is left-handed and he writes in old-world French script. He rides in a carriage with a driver, so he has an accomplice," Edge told him. "That's not much to go on," the captain told him. One thing is bothering me, though, Edge." "What's that, Captain?" he asked. The captain looked at Edge and asked him, "What does the term 'fubar' mean? "I never heard of a cop that didn't know that before, but it means 'Fucked Up Beyond All Recognition" Edge smiled at him and left the office with a wide grin on his face. The captain shook his head from side to side as he seemed sorry he had asked Edge the question. Edge had always been a smart ass and why would he change now.

Edge sat at Abbie's desk and again went through all the research she had done, most of it on Jack the Ripper. She had books written about him, and fiction stories also. She had computer printouts about the similarities of the cases, even astrological signs highlighting the facets of the moon. This approach seemed interesting to him as it was beginning to make sense. He kept reading her notes on the cases, and in each murder the moon was full and it was cool outside. He was trying to figure out where the fog came into the picture as it seemed when she came up missing, there was a fog. He came to the conclusion that the fog was the killer's cover and no one would be suspicious as to what the fog really meant. There was a note on Abbie's her desk to call an Inspector Huntington at Scotland Yard ASAP. Edge looked at his watch and decided to give the inspector a call. Edge asked the operator for a long-distance line and to connect him with Scotland Yard. A tiny squeaky voice on the other end answered and said, "Scotland Yard, how may I direct your call?" in her sexiest British accent. "Inspector Hunnington, please. This is Lt. Neil Woodredge in the United States." "Just a minute. I'll connect you," the voice said. Edge was listening and thinking about what he was going to say to the inspector. The inspector came on the line and the conversation started. "Inspector Hunnington here, chap. How is everything in America, old boy?" Edge was taken aback for a second there because he wasn't used to being called an old boy or a chap. "Everything is fine in America, but not in Niagara Falls, Inspector. This is Lt. Neil Woodredge of the Falls Police Department. I understand my partner Detective Abigail Cook called to talk to you about a murder case we are working on." "Yes, I do recollect a message here to call her, but I'm afraid I received no answer from her, so I let it pass, my friend," the inspector told him. "Well, my friend, I'm calling you, and I would like to get to the root of my problem here, OK? It seems we have three dead hookers here, brutalized beyond recognition, and we have reason to believe that Jack the Ripper is behind these killings." As Edge listened into the receiver, all he heard was laughter, and his patience was running thin with this English muffin. Finally after the laughter died down, the inspector came back on the line with his normal tone. "That's impossible. The ripper's been dead these many years, old chap." "Hey, look it here, English muffin, my partner is in the hospital because she has seen and met the ripper. What do you have to say about that, old chap?" Edge said sarcastically. Silence was what he heard for a few seconds, and then the inspector's reply was, "Send me everything you have on the murders, and I will send you everything I have on the Jack the Ripper case. Agreed lieutenant?" "Very well, Inspector. I'll fax everything I have on our murders. I'll be expecting yours as well. Thank you, Inspector." "Obliged to help in anyway I can lieutenant." The phone conversation was over and Edge gathered up everything and went to the fax machine.

Chapter Thirteen

Inspector Hunnington of Scotland Yard sent a fax to Edge explaining that he would receive the ripper files via FedEx Air, since there was too much information to be sent by a fax machine. Edge returned the same message. Captain Eckersley came over to Abbie's desk where Edge had taken over and told Edge that Inspector Hunnington had called and requested permission to fly to the United States and be a part of the investigation. Captain Eckersley was all for it, since the inspector was a seasoned veteran of Scotland Yard and was very familiar with the ripper case there. Scotland Yard took the ripper case seriously because he was never caught. Edge looked up at the captain with a disgusted expression. "Look it, Captain, I don't like that cheeky fellow." "Well, when he arrives, you will pick him up at the airport and work with him. You never know, he may have different ideas. Besides, it's like a vacation to him." "When is he arriving?" Edge asked. "This evening at Buffalo/ Niagara Airport at nine. You can't miss him; he has a handlebar mustache and graying hair. He is a short fella. Just put a sign in front of you, and he will see you," Captain Eckersley explained. Edge continued to browse the evidence, ignoring the captain's big frame in front of him. When the captain left, Edge muttered "smashing" to himself and wondered where the captain kept his brains. Probably on the seat of his pants, glued to his office chair. Edge told Reyes that the inspector was coming to Niagara Falls to observe the case. Reyes rolled his eyes, since detectives do not like their toes stepped on by anyone, especially a cheeky fellow from England.

Tonight was a special night; the moon would be full and a winter snowfall would be beginning the season of a cold, snow-filled winter. The Farmers' Almanac said it would be a very bad winter this year, with much lake-effect snow. This would not help in the investigation. Sometimes winters in the Niagara area could be brutal, since there is Lake Erie on one side and Lake Ontario on the other. Edge knew it wouldn't deter Jack from doing his butchery. He had seen many murders in his days on the force, but none as bad as this. He kept thinking to himself that this guy has to make a mistake sometime, and Edge will be right there to take him out. He wanted him so badly; he could taste the English muffin melt in his mouth. He had to think like him and be him. What would Jack the Ripper do? Even if it wasn't him, what would the killer do? Edge thought for a moment and came to the conclusion that he would continue to hunt down hookers and pick them off one by one. Edge had set up a surveillance in an area where he figured Jack would strike next—a high-hooker area or a high-drug area where hookers congregate so they can get easy access to drugs. So he chose Pierce Avenue and Thirteenth Street, but first he had to see Abbie.

Edge left the station, got into his unmarked, and headed for the hospital, since he had a few hours to kill before getting to the airport to pick up the inspector. The air was cold, and the heater wasn't the best in his car, so he had to make the best of it. His body was getting the chills from the late afternoon air. Maybe when the car warmed up, the chills would go away. Pulling out of the police parking lot, he headed toward Walnut Avenue. He had to stop at his apartment before visiting Abbie to pick up a pack of smokes and a change of clothes. When he arrived at his place, the owner of a local eatery was out front arguing with a customer over the bill. Edge exited the vehicle, and Larry, the owner, called to him, "Hey Edge, come here a minute, will you please?" "What's up, Larry?" Edge asked, "Got a problem?" "Yes, sir," Larry said, "This guy won't pay his bill for the food he ordered." Edge looked at the man who was very inebriated and asked him what his problem was. The man stated, "I didn't like the fucking food, man." Edge continued to look at him and said, "But you ate the fucking food, didn't you, dickhead." "Ya, I ate it, but I ain't paying for it and I ain't no dickhead," said he the man as he took a swing at Edge, who avoided the blow and threw the man up against the car, face smashing into the hood, causing his nose to spew blood all over Edge's car. Edge cuffed the irate customer as the man protested loudly that he was unaware that Edge was a cop. Edge held him, frisked him, and then looked at Larry and asked him, "How much does this joker owe you for the food?" "$10.55," was Larry's reply. Edge reached into the drunk's pocket, retrieved twelve dollars, and gave it to Larry along with a tip. Larry acknowledged with a thank you and went back to his place of business. Edge put the drunk in the back of his car, while he went upstairs to get what he needed. With the drunk protesting again and banging his head up against the car window, Edge thought maybe he would knock himself silly and sleep it off in the car. Edge returned a moment later and was right—the drunk had knocked himself unconscious. Edge then drove over to see Abbie.

When Edge entered Abbie's room, she was sitting up in bed and smiled as he came in the room. He bent over, gave her a kiss, and asked her, "How is it going, babe? "I feel a lot better now that you're here," she replied. "You look a lot better than when I brought you in," he said to her. "So, how is the case coming along?" she asked him. "Well that's what I want to talk to you about, if you feel up to it. I contacted Scotland Yard and they're sending an inspector here to observe. They had a good laugh when I told them that Jack the Ripper was here killing hookers." Edge laughed. "He is here and I met him. I was in his carriage and spoke with him. He is tall and handsome with mesmerizing eyes—like hypnotic ones. You look at him, and he puts you in a trance-like state—you're not in control of your actions. That's how he got me to take the arsenic," Abbie continued telling Edge about everything that happened while she was in the carriage and under the ripper's spell. She explained to Edge that he went by the name John. Edge listened tentatively to everything she said—her whole ordeal. Edge looked at her with much concern, and everything she said seemed to stay in line with evidence they had collected already. He wanted this guy more and more as she spoke, because she was his woman and he wanted revenge at all costs, even if it meant his job. Finally she added that she realized why she was still alive. She was a police officer, and for some reason or another, he didn't kill cops. Edge peered out the window and realized it was snowing lightly. He looked at Abbie and told her it was snowing—big flakes. He turned around and saw her smiling as he lifted himself out of the chair and walked to the window. She knew he was upset. "Come here, sweetheart," she said. "I know I've been through a lot in the last week or so, but I'm fine. I think you know how I feel about you, and I have always felt that way. Nothing's changed, not even when you were on suspension." Edge looked at her, noting the tears welling from her eyes. He sat on the bed and said to her, "I think you know too." Edge leaned into her and gave her a long, passionate kiss. "I gotta go and pick up this English muffin at the airport. I'll see you later," He said as he got up to leave the room. Standing at her door, she called to him. "I love you, Edge," she said. He turned to her and told her, "Don't get emotional on me, Abbie. I need a tough broad," he laughed as he left, walking down the hallway; there was a tear in the corner of his eye. He entered the elevator and realized he had a prisoner in the back of his unmarked. The drunk was awake when he arrived at the car, and he noticed Edge walking his way. He started shouting profanities at him, so Edge opened the door, dragged him out of the car, opened the trunk, and shoved him in it while he was still cursing him. Closing the trunk lid and listening to the man pounding on the underside, screaming to be let out, Edge said, "When you learn to behave and stop this nonsense, I'll think about letting you out." Edge got in the driver's side, started the engine, and continued down Tenth Street toward Buffalo Avenue to the Grand Island Bridge to Buffalo/Niagara airport. He had an hour to get there before the inspector's flight arrived.

Chapter Fourteen

Edge arrived at Buffalo/Niagara Airport twenty minutes before the inspector's flight was due to land. The drunken man was still in the trunk, but not as loud as he once was. Edge pounded on the lid of the trunk, waiting for a reply. None came. He opened the trunk and there, staring at him, was the misbehaving man. "Are you going to behave yourself?" Edge asked him. "You're a fucking asshole," he said, "You know that." Edge didn't let him finish what he was saying and slammed the lid. "I guess not," Edge shook his head smiling. Edge went into the airport, leaving the man screaming in the trunk. It was cold in the trunk, but Edge didn't care, figuring the cold air would sober him up faster. Edge walked to the terminal with his sign and waited at the gate for Inspector Hunnington's plane. It was 8:50 p.m., and the flight sign lit up as being on time. "Hardly," Edge thought. He never knew flights to be on time anywhere. When he flew, it was never on time. 'Course that was his luck always. That's why he didn't like flying. He walked to the information station and asked the customer service representative about the flight. She explained to him that it was scheduled to be on time. Instead of going back to his seat, he proceeded to the snack bar to get a cup of coffee. The snack bar was closed. The lady told him to get a cup from the coffee vending machine. He went to the machine, inserted his coins, and a cup dropped, filled with hot black coffee. He took the cup and sipped it slowly, since it was very hot. It was now after nine, and he was right again—the flights were never on time. Fifteen minutes later, passengers started coming out of the plane, so he raised his sign at them to see which one would acknowledge him. They all shook their heads from side to side in a "no" motion. Finally a gray-haired man walked up to him and introduced himself as Inspector Gerard Hunnington. "You must be Lieutenant Woodredge?" he asked. "They call me Edge," he retorted. "Well, they call me Inspector Hunnington, not English muffin," as the sign that Edge was holding said. "Now that pleasantries are out of the way, I think I'll resolve to my hotel room for much-needed rest to be rid of this jet lag," the inspector looked at Edge, "You do have a room for me, don't you, young fellow?" "I'll set you up at the Quality Inn, if that's all right?" Edge asked. "Anywhere that has a nice breakfast and tea will be fine, thank you, Sledge," he chuckled as he grabbed his luggage and continued walking away from Edge. Edge followed him down the walkway toward the exit door. Exiting the airport and waiting on Edge to catch up, the inspector looked around at the traffic cruising past and taxi cabs dropping off passengers and picking up people getting off their flights. "I said they call me Edge, not Sledge or anything else, OK Teacake? Now let's go. The car is over here." Inspector Hunnington now followed Edge to where he had parked the car. They both got to the car at about the same time, and the drunk was still yelling from the trunk. "Who's in the trunk?" the inspector asked. "No one important," Edge came back. "They sure do things differently in America," continued the inspector. Edge drove the inspector to the Quality Inn at downtown Niagara Falls and checked him in under the city's tab. The inspector went to his room with Edge in tow, and opened his door with the electronic key. On opening the door, his eyes followed all around the room; he opened the closet door and then peered into the bathroom. A queen-sized bed was in the center of the room, facing the television, with twin nightstands on each side with a lamp on each one. "Comfy," the inspector said. "I'm glad it meets with your approval," Edge said to him. "May I ask something of you, Sledge, I mean, Edge? "What do you want now?" Edge looked irritated. "Would you be so kind as to direct me to Niagara Falls?" Inspector Hunnington asked. "This is Niagara Falls. You're here," Edge came back. "No, I mean the overflow of water itself—I hear it is spectacular anytime of the year." "OK Hunnington, let's go. Hop in the car. I'll show it to you." As Edge left the room ahead of the inspector, he said to himself, "Now I'm a fucking tour guide." They got into the car and drove toward Goat Island and over the bridge, stopping at the top overlooking the rapids flowing fast to the brink of the falls. "This is magnificent—what a view, lieutenant," the inspector said. Driving further down the road to the entrance of the Bridal Veil Falls, Edge parked the car and they walked down the steps through the falling snow to the railing of the falls. The inspector looked across to the Canadian side, and to the left were the Horseshoe Falls. He also could see the Rainbow Bridge. "This is a spectacle in itself, Edge," Inspector H. Said, "I will have to stay longer to absorb all of this beauty and splendor." "Stay as long as you like, Inspector," Edge told him. "What is that area over across the water, on the other side?" he asked. "That's Canada over there," explained Edge. "Marvelous, just marvelous—Canada and America bordering one another," Inspector H. replied excitedly. "It's the longest-running peacekeeping border in the history of the world," Edge told him, looking bored. "I find it simply astonishing. I think I will have to come back and shoot some flicks of the area—the falls and the lower part of the river. Well, I think it's time we say hidey ho before that bloke freezes in the trunk of your motor vehicle, Edge," the inspector sounded sympathetic. "He won't freeze. He has so much alcohol in him—that's all he needs to keep warm," Edge looked at him warningly. They returned to Edge's car without saying a word. Once inside, they could still hear the protests of the drunk in the trunk. The inspector looked at Edge and then around the beautiful scenery surrounding the park and the rapids as they drove out of Niagara's Goat Island Park toward the Quality Inn. On the way, the inspector was full of questions, but hesitated asking Edge anything, figuring Edge was in a bad mood. He sat there in the car thinking about the nice, colorful lights illuminating the Niagara and Horseshoe Falls. Arriving at the Quality Inn, the inspector exited the vehicle and turned to Edge, "I guess I'll see you in the a.m., huh old chap." Edge nodded in agreement, not liking it one bit, but he knew he had orders to work with the man. "Toota-loo, lieutenant. Good night," said Inspector Hunnington. Edge drove away, his tires squealing all the way down Second Street. The drunk in the trunk continued his protesting, so Edge fishtailed his car so the drunk would roll about in the trunk. The man in the trunk decided to keep quiet until Edge let him out, as he was beginning to sober up. Edge's driving definitely had an impact on his disposition. Edge continued down Rainbow Boulevard to Tenth Street, where he pulled up to a group of individuals hanging out on the corner of Tenth and Niagara Streets. "Where is Tina?" Edge asked the group. One man came forward—a tall, black man with dreadlocks—who seemed to be the spokesman for the group, and told Edge he saw Tina hanging around at Nineteenth and Niagara at the laundromat. Edge nodded his appreciation and drove onto Nineteenth and Niagara. Slowing down, he looked on all corners, but found no trace of Tina. He even stepped into the laundromat; there was only one old sider doing her clothes there. Edge thought maybe she had a trick and the trick took her a safe place to have a good time. Edge was unaware that the moon was full and John was out prowling for his next victim—Tina.

John had Tina in his carriage and knew she was going to be easy prey, since she smoked crack just a few moments before she stepped into his carriage. When John offered her the arsenic, it was probably the easiest prey he had ever had. She took it without hesitation and right up her nose in a deep snort. Immediately she was out cold with the crack high and the poison. John didn't care whether she was still breathing or not because he was just beginning. His carriage was crossing the bridge at Duck Island at Hyde Park Lake. Angus climbed down and helped him with Tina's unconscious body. John and Angus placed her limp body in the middle of the pavilion, Angus then returned to the carriage. John removed his blades from a case he was carrying and removed a large knife as he prepared to open her up. He slit her throat from ear to ear first, blood gurgling in her throat and exiting the artery in various directions. He inserted the knife just below the breastbone in a downward slice to her pubic area, exposing her abdominal area. Then he removed her liver and placed it in a wooden box, which he set aside. Laughing uncontrollably, he proceeded to cut up her face. He then took a smaller blade—a scalpel by appearance, and carved the name Jack just above her breasts. Pleased with his recent work, he returned to the carriage with the liver in the box. Angus slapped the reins and the horses started to turn around to exit the park.

Edge returned to the police headquarters, got out of the car, went to the back, and opened the trunk to a much disgruntled and sober man. Helping him out, Edge looked at him and said, "Had enough or would you like to stay as a guest of the city for the night?" The man, with tears in his eyes and blood still on his nose, mumbled an apology. Edge unlocked the handcuffs and put them in his holder. The now sober man, rubbing his wrists, looked at Edge. "What happens now?" he asked. "You can go now," Edge told him, "but don't let me catch you drunk and disorderly again. If you order food and eat it, you had better pay the bill, understand asshole?" The man nodded and walked away with a "thank you very much" look on his face. Edge watched the man walk down Hyde Park Boulevard. He thought to himself, "This must be the stupid people day." Edge got into his private vehicle, which was a broken-down rust bucket of a Pontiac GTO. He drove onto Hyde Park Boulevard toward Niagara Street to try and locate Tina. He had some questions he needed to ask her, unaware that she was already a victim of John's deadly rampage. Turning right onto Niagara, he arrived at her usual corner, but to no avail—there was no Tina anywhere. He proceeded to the hospital to spend the rest of his night with Abbie. In the morning he had to pick up the Englishman and head to the office to meet with the captain. He parked out front of the hospital and took the elevator to the third floor, walking into Abbie's room; she was there sleeping peacefully. He sat down in the chair by her bed, and his mind was clouded by sleep. Meanwhile John was preparing another delivery, this time to a different party—Abbie Cook.

Chapter Fifteen

Abbie awoke to a loud, obnoxious sound coming from the window side of her room where Edge was sitting in the chair—legs crossed, arms folded, snoring away in dreamland. She picked up a small box of facial tissue and threw it in his direction, hitting him in the head, waking him suddenly in the middle of a deep snore. He jumped and went for his weapon, his left hand grasping the pistol grip. "What cha' going to do, shoot me?" she asked him. "The thought crossed my mind more than once, you know," he said sleepily. "How are you feeling, Abbie?" Edge asked. "I'm ready to get the hell out of here and back to work. I'm supposed to go home today, hopefully soon." "Well, I think maybe I'll try to hurry things along, you know, with my usual charming self," Edge laughed. Edge went out to the nurse's station, and to his astonishment, there was nurse bitch. Edge decided to let Abbie check out herself instead of dealing with this woman. Edge returned to Abbie and told her she would have to wait for the doctor to discharge her probably sometime after breakfast. She decided to shower and then eat breakfast, since she didn't have much of an appetite anyway. The sooner she was out of the hospital, the better she would be. She missed being on the case. Edge heard the water running in the shower and his evil, filthy mind went to work. He entered the shower room and removed his clothing, stepping into the shower with Abbie who became alarmed. "What the . . ." she was cut short when Edge put his arms around her and began to passionately kiss her. Her hands began to massage his back and his chest as she returned his kiss in kind. His hands were gripping her buttocks, lifting her up as she was wrapping her legs around him in heated passion. He entered her zone of love, and she gave a slight squeal. He hushed her a little, and their lovemaking was hot and heavy. He pinned her against the shower wall, and his hips were moving rapidly, giving her much pleasure. Her quick and heavy breathing set him on fire. "Oh! Oh! My . . . ," and then one last "Oh my God" as their bodies convulsed in ecstasy. Now with their love session over, it was time to get showered and dressed, neither one saying anything, just smiling at one another. Edge left the shower and toweled off, leaving Abbie to dry her hair and get dressed. As Edge was dressing, Nurse Smith came in the room and noticed Edge in his birthday suit. Edge had the towel in front of him and addressed Nurse Bitch, "I guess you could say you caught me with my pants down." He had a shit-eating grin on his face. "Lieutenant Woodredge, this is a hospital, not a bordello," she yelled at him. "Oh, pipe down nurse, I only took a shower." his grin continuing to show, because he and Abbie were the only ones who knew what went on as the nurse was only speculating. "Now be a good little nurse and get the doctor so we get out of here. I have to pick someone up in an hour or so." "With pleasure," she said. Edge smiled and said, "That's already been taken care of, thank you." Appalled, she left the room. Abbie finished breakfast and a hospitalist came in and examined her, giving her a clean bill of health. Her discharge was waiting.

Edge and Abbie left the hospital and gladly got into Edge's squad car, driving off to the Quality Inn to pick up Inspector Hunnington. The inspector was waiting in the lobby as Edge walked up to him. "Ready to go, Inspector?" Edge asked. "By all means, old chap, I am definitely bloody ready. I have been bloody ready for over an hour," he retorted at edge, an uneasy tone in his voice. "I'm not one for being on time, cheeky fellow," Edge shot back. Inspector Hunnington sat in the back, and Edge introduced Abbie to him. They both shook hands with pleasurable greetings. Edge explained to the inspector what happened to Abbie and that he had to pick her up at the hospital. The inspector nodded apologetically. They all drove to the police station, only to stop at Starbucks for a morning cup of java. The inspector seemed to be taking a liking to American coffee. Arriving at the headquarters, the trio headed to Captain Eckersley's office. When Abbie walked in, the other detectives swarmed her with hugs and kisses, welcoming her back with a ton of questions. Captain Eckersley noticed the commotion and yelled from his office, "OK people, let's get back to work. We can get re-acquainted after hours." Abbie, Edge, and Inspector Hunnington entered the captain's office, closing the door behind them. Edge introduced Captain Eckersley to Inspector Hunnington of Scotland Yard. The captain went through the rhetoric of the case with the trio so the inspector could be totally filled in. "So, you think you have the original Jack the Ripper here in Niagara Falls?" the inspector inquired. The captain was now standing at the window of his office, peering at the traffic driving by. His head turned to look at the inspector with piercing eyes, as if they were lasers about to zap him into oblivion or through the door which he came through. Detective Cook broke the silence and said, "I don't think its Jack the Ripper, I know it is. I met him and spoke to him in his carriage. He hypnotized me somehow, and drugged me and left me in an alley. He so much as told me who he was. I remember his cold, dark stare as he looked into my eyes and spoke to me. He was a very well-spoken, eloquent, and distinguishable sort of gentleman. He even tipped his hat as he introduced himself. He appeared to be tall and dark-haired, with a thin build. He had a mustache and goatee, very neat in appearance. He had a dark suit with a red tie, and the tie clasp had a "J" on it.

It wasn't exactly a tie, but a kerchief or a scarf around his neck. He wore a black cape with a red lining in it. His boots were black and well-shined. His carriage was black and had red velvet interior—very well maintained. There were two horses pulling the carriage. There was a driver whose name I don't recollect." "Is there anything else you can remember about that night?" the inspector asked. "Yes, He called me a bobby, an inspector to be precise." The captain and the inspector listened to Detective Cook tentatively. Edge had heard all of this before, and so he knew not to comment on anything of the sort. He sat there and let Abbie bring everyone up-to-date on what happened to her that night. The inspector had a serious look in his eyes, one that could only be described as bewildered as he listened to every word. "Maybe you have a copycat murderer here, making it look like a Jack the Ripper crime." The inspector chimed in, "No! It was him, I tell you. He calls himself John, but most people refer to him as Jack. That's what he told me. One other thing that I forgot to mention—the name on the side of the carriage was "Cobblestone Carriage Company." The inspector's eyes grew as wide as silver dollars, since no one knew of that part of the investigation. The inspector knew what they were dealing with, and it wasn't a copycat killer. Captain Eckersley interjected and told Abbie she would have to work with the department's sketch artist, and maybe they could come up with something similar to show the inspector. Detective Cook left the meeting and headed to the police sketch lab. The captain looked at Edge and the inspector, "Well what you deduce from what you heard already?" Inspector Hunnington said, "You do have a sort of a dilemma here, but The Ripper, I doubt it very much." "You heard what Cook said, Hunnington—she saw and met Jack the Ripper," Edge stared at him as if to say to him, "You're full of shit." "If she said those things, then they are true. Let me show you the evidence we have collected, and you go over it and give us you're analogy of the crimes." Edge left with the inspector, they went to Edge's desk where all the ripper's evidence was, and the inspector began to read the statements and investigative reports. He put on his reading spectacles and started at the first murder, glancing occasionally at Edge, who seemed disinterested at his being here. The captain motioned Edge to his office, and Edge reluctantly went in. "So, what do you think of this Englishman, Edge?" "I think he knows more than he's telling us. Did you see his eyes when Abbie mentioned the writing on the side of the carriage? He definitely knows what we're dealing with here." "Well, keep him on the case and keep him busy and updated on everything pertaining to the ripper investigation." Edge began to leave the captain's office, when the phone rang and the captain held up his forefinger as if to tell Edge to hold on a minute. He put the phone back on its cradle and told Edge they found another body—a black female. Edge was hoping it wasn't Tina. Edge headed to Hyde Park Lake with Inspector Hunnington in tow.

Chapter Sixteen

Detective Cook was sitting next to Sgt. Adrian Jackson, giving details of John's facial features, making various changes in the nose and eye area, and a little chin change here and a cheek change there. All in all, it came out pretty close as she remembered him. When Sergeant Jackson was finished, Abbie cried out, "That's him!" Sergeant Jackson gazed at the eyes of the picture she drew of John and noticed how they would appear in person. "He is a handsome devil, isn't he, Abbie?' "The devil is exactly what he is, Adrian. If you ever see this man, run for the hills and hide," Abbie told her. Abbie left her office and headed for the squad room with the sketch in hand. She needed to show it to Inspector Hunnington right away. Entering the squad room, Abbie went directly to the captain's office and handed it to him immediately. "So, this is our Jack the Ripper? He doesn't look like much to me," he said as he looked at Abbie. "Believe me, Captain; he looks a lot scarier in person," she exclaimed. "Where are the inspector and Edge?" she asked. "They are on the scene of our latest homicide, Detective," Captain Eckersley said. "Why am I out?" Detective Cook asked him. "You've been traumatized enough, Detective. I would like you to relax a little before you get any more involved." There was a kindness being shown in his eyes that the Detective hadn't noticed before—a kind of caring aura about him. "Is there anything else I can do for you, Detective?" he looked at her like a concerned father. "No, sir," she answered back. "Well, get your chicken ass outta here and back to your desk," he commanded. "Yes, sir!" came her reply. "He cares," she thought to herself, smiling all the way to her desk. She sat down and glanced around the room and back at the captain's office. He was standing at the window, wiping his eyes with a snot-stained handkerchief. She knew deep down he had a human side to him, but he had to be a cop first.

Edge and the inspector arrived on Duck Island, only to be met by two fishermen who discovered the body. The body was placed in the middle of the pavilion with the arms outstretched and legs together; the ankles were crossed over one another. The face was badly mutilated and the abdomen was open and eviscerated. The legs were bound with raw hide. This was different than the other four. The CSI's arrived, and Charlie was the first to speak with Edge. "This is number 4, Charlie," Edge told him. "Do your thing, my friend. This is

Inspector Hunnington from Scotland Yard," he said as he introduced Charlie and the inspector. They shook hands and exchanged pleasantries. Both watched as Charlie and crew taped off the area to ward off any reporters who might get wind of this latest murder. Charlie knelt down, took out a thermometer, and inserted the pointed end into the liver. It came out to be a cold eighty-three degrees. "She been dead I'd say about twenty-four to forty-eight hours, give or take," Charlie looked up at Edge and Inspector Hunnington, "Rigor already set in." "Hey Charlie, check out the legs. They're crossed and tied together," Edge informed him. "This is different than the others we encountered," Charlie surmised. Charlie proceeded to cut the raw hide and place it in a plastic evidence bag. "Look between the legs, into her vaginal cavity, and see what's in there. It seems like a piece of paper of some sorts." the inspector noted. Charlie began to do what the inspector asked, and lo and behold, there was a piece of paper there folded in quarters. Charlie removed the blood-stained paper and unfolded it. It was a note from the killer, written in old-style French script. It read as follows:

> *Dear Abbie,*
>
> *This one's for you, my lady. You can't catch me. You can't catch me. You can't catch me. You will never catch me. I will send you the part I like best.*
>
> *Yours Always, J.*

The note seemed to be written on the same old-style stationary as the other writings. Charlie put the paper in an evidence bag to check for prints, which he wouldn't find any. He hadn't found any as of yet—this guy was careful. Charlie looked at Edge and then the inspector. "What do you make of this, Inspector?" Edge asked him. "You have an interesting case here, lieutenant. I'd say you have a ripper on your hands. By the looks of things, he is one nasty goomer. He's not an English muffin by any means. He's a cruel and sadistic bastard," said Inspector Hunnington. "Is it the real, authentic Jack the Ripper?" Edge asked him. "It appears to be his workmanship," the inspector said in a sad voice. Edge bent down with Charlie and told him, "I need all the evidence I can get to catch this guy. Go over everything with a fine-tooth comb. I know what killed her—I mean, her cause of death. I need something extra, and I don't care if you have to work overtime. This guy has made a challenge to us that we can't catch him. It's a personal vendetta now." "Right, Edge, I will let you know what I find," Charlie told him. Charlie continued to mark up blood splatter and take samples as Edge and his new partner—not to his liking, of course—were interviewing the fishermen. It seems the fishermen only came across her when they were going to sit at the picnic table for lunch. There wasn't much new to the case as there were no witnesses again. Charlie caught Edge and the inspector before they headed out to write the reports on the corpse. "I made an error in the temperature of the body. Upon further examination of the body, it seems there is no liver, so the temp is null and void. Still she has been dead a day or so. Cause of death is the slicing of the throat, causing her to bleed out. The killer took her liver as the trophy. It appears that everything else is intact." "Thanks, Charlie," Edge said. "Inspector Hunnington, do you feel like a liver and onions dinner?" Edge asked laughing. "Your chuckles are not welcome at this time, Woodredge—it's a poor state of humor. That was a live human being a couple of days ago, and you have to make liver quips when hers is missing," Inspector Hunnington seemed to be counseling him on etiquette. "Life is a bitch, ain't it? Then you kick the bucket and it's all over. Got what I'm saying, Hunnington?" Edge stated to him. "I got your bloody message, Edge. I got your bloody message."

Edge and the inspector left the scene as Charlie and his team bagged the body and shoved it in the body wagon. All the way back to the station, the inspector was speechless. "You don't like me too much, do you, Inspector?" Edge asked him. "What gave you that dizzy notion, Woodredge?" the inspector came back with his own question. "You're silent. You haven't been silent since you arrived stateside. It's all you have done is flap your trap constantly. It must be in your blood. Now you don't say a word. That's odd, don't you think?" Edge continued. "I'm thinking about the case at hand, and I suggest you do the same," Inspector Hunnington looked out the window of the vehicle at what was left of the snow, listening to sounds of the vehicle sloshing through the wet street. He knew it was Jack the Ripper. But how was this possible? How did he get here? These questions had to be answered. He had once read a book by H. G. Wells titled "The Time Machine." It was about time travel. Could Jack the Ripper be traveling back through time? It was a distinct possibility, but an improbable one.

Edge dropped Inspector Hunnington off at the headquarters and headed toward Goat Island. On the way, he stopped and grabbed a bologna-and-onions sandwich at Greasy Spoon on Third Street, along with a beer. He used his badge to get free parking and parked along the swift-moving rapids. He exited the vehicle and started walking down the path to the Bridal Veil Falls, all along thinking about the case and the dead girls. Four dead girls and one almost-dead detective. If she hadn't been a cop, it would be five. It seemed he wasn't after cops, and that was a good thing. Prostitutes were his main objective. But why? Edge's thoughts were racing through his head, all the while forgetting about his bologna-and-onions sandwich with mustard. He was overlooking the falls and listening to its roar as the water pounded the rocks below. His thoughts changed to the people who committed suicide by jumping the guardrail and plummeting to their deaths at the hands of the jagged rocks sitting below the overflowing water, tons of water smashing their frail bodies—some staying awhile and others moving along the white water, only to be spotted by fishermen or boaters. Then the rescue team would have to take over and retrieve them. It was a costly job. He finally realized he had a sandwich—which was now cold—opened it and chopped a bite, dripping mustard down his shirt. He looked down and thought to himself what a slob he was. He had heard that before from Cook. She was always calling him a slob. He considered himself a heathen and wiped his hands on his pants even though he was offered a napkin. Edge cracked open the beer and took a swallow, which went down smooth. The seagulls were flying low and some landing a safe distance from him, not getting to close for he could be a predator. He broke off a piece of bread, threw it in the middle of the pack, and watched as they fought over the morsel. Screeching a "thank you" was their way of communicating to him and asking for more. He turned his attention to the Canadian side, chomping down some more sandwich and taking a drink of beer to wash it down. He couldn't believe how gorgeous it was over there, and how natural it was on this side. It was more commercialized in Canada, and the Canadian government seemed to offer more to the tourists. He looked at the falls and then at the seagulls who were waiting for more of his lunch. He finished his beer and tossed what was left of his sandwich to the gulls. They gobbled it up and flew away again, screeching their appreciation. Edge kept the bottle and placed it in his jacket pocket, since it was worth a five cent piece. That would be five cents the crackheads wouldn't get. He felt relaxed being near the falls. He always did his best thinking at the falls. He came to the conclusion that Jack was like the seagulls in a way, being close, but not to close. He had to figure out how Jack was getting here and where his next appearance would be. Maybe Edge would throw him a piece of bread and see where he would come to gobble it up.

Chapter Seventeen

Detective Cook and Inspector Hunnington were sitting at the conference room table with papers spread out all over the table, discussing the case of the ripper. It seemed there were similarities among the girls. They were all killed when there was a full moon. They were all prostitutes, maybe barring one, which was Tammie Martin. She had a clean police record. But Jack didn't know that. He mistook her for one. They were killed under the cover of fog. The weather reports in England at the time of each murder stated storm and rain. Thunder and lightning with a mix of high humidity would produce a fog-like effect. When would he strike next? Probably the next full moon with a thunder storm. Their concentration was interrupted by Detective Reyes who opened the door and peered in. "Hey Abbie, you have a package on your desk" he said. "Where did it come from?" she asked. "No return address on it," he explained. "OK, Reyes. Thanks a lot." Abbie looked at the inspector and they both rose from their seats at the same time. She got to her desk first, and they both gazed at the package. She took out a pair of surgical gloves from her desk drawer, as well as a pen knife and a pair of tweezers. Carefully slicing the tape which held it together and using the tweezers to separate the paper, she moved the paper down the side of the box. She had a feeling what was inside the box. It was the same type of box that Jack had used before, with the cigar company logo on it. Flipping the clasp and opening the lid, she noticed an object wrapped in paper—newspaper to be exact. On unraveling the paper, to their astonishment they saw that it was a human liver. Abbie moved away from it as if it might be diseased or an alien. Inspector Hunnington looked a little puzzled, as if he was hiding a secret. She looked at him and said, "What do you know about this, Inspector?" "I knew he was going to send you this, but I didn't know when. He left a note in the vagina of the last victim stating he was going to send you his favorite part. I didn't tell you because I didn't want to upset you. I'm sorry." "That's all right, Inspector. I kinda figured I was going to be his center of attention. So far, I'm the only one, who has seen him and can identify him, still alive. It was just a little shocking, is all. I'm OK. Let's get this to the lab and see whose liver it is, and see if we can get prints from any of the paper or the box. I don't believe so, but we have to cover all bases. The detective squad room went back to order as Reyes put on some gloves and carried the box and its wrappings to the crime lab. Cook and Hunnington went back to the conference room. Captain Eckersley looked curiously at Detective Cook, making sure of her composure.

Edge entered the squad room and went directly to the conference room, where Hunnington and Cook were reviewing evidence. "Hey Edge," Abbie said as he opened the door. "Whats up, love? And how about you mate?" Edge said with a snicker. The inspector just looked at Edge with no emotion or acknowledgement. He continued to write on his yellow tablet. "We have been finalizing evidence. What have you been doing?" Abbie asked. "I've been feeding the seagulls and drinking beer. That's what I've been doing," Edge explained. Abbie told him about the package and its contents. Edge just looked at her as if he didn't know. She returned the female look she always did when she knew he was lying or was about too. They explained to him what they had found similar about all the murders. He acknowledged by nodding his head. After they were through talking, Edge told them how the seagulls had given him an idea on how to find Jack the Ripper. He explained to them that the ripper was closer than they thought. They just had to bait him better. "Have we received any info from the RAC patrol?" Edge asked. "No," Abbie said, "They're busy trying to keep the hookers inside, so we don't have any more victims." "Well, arrest them all! The sooner the better. Put them in protective custody. The less hookers that are out there, the less targets he has. If they don't want to stay inside on their own, then make them stay in as our guests. Just until we get him or keep him from coming back. It will only be a few days or so." They all nodded in agreement. They would bring it to the captain's attention.

Inspector Hunnington was on the phone with Scotland Yard, inquiring about the next full moon and the weather reports in London for the next week. He had his own thoughts about catching the ripper. His interpretation of the evidence concluded that Jack the Ripper was entering this century through a vortex or a door to the future from his time. The thunder, lightning, and 100 percent humidity, along with the changing timetable of the moon, would cause a portal to open, and then Jack would come through to this century. What he had to figure out was where Jack would come through on this side, and also, where he would enter through the portal in his time frame. It seemed to be just a freak of nature in the weather patterns. He figured he had Jack right where he wanted him. It seemed the most logical place he would enter was at the falling water between the two countries. Now where would he enter from his side? It is concluded that Jack the Ripper did most of his murders in the White Chapel area of London, so this would be the logical choice of area he would come through to this side. He would have to bring this theory to the attention of Edge and Detective Cook in the presence of Captain Eckersley. He didn't think that the duo would buy the theory on their own. They would have their doubts because he was a foreigner, and their pride as police officers would be tarnished by an outsider, even though he was an authority on Jack the Ripper. He studied the ripper case files as a hobby, as did every other inspector at Scotland Yard. Jack the Ripper was never caught, and there have been many theories on his identity and what happened to him. It seems the ripper not only killed in England, but also in Scotland and Ireland. Maybe he traveled this way also in his own time. Maybe he figured a way to be at the right place at the right time to transport him from one country to another. The theory could be made practical if he could prove it. He needed to be alone to write a report to Captain Eckersley.

Inspector Hunnington asked Edge to drive him back to his hotel room for the evening, and Edge was pleased to oblige him. They got into Edge's car; he inserted the key and turned it, listening to the engine come to life. He pulled out onto Hyde Park Boulevard to Walnut Avenue as he did many times. Making a left onto Walnut Avenue, the inspector opened the conversation, "Apologies to you, Edge, for the silent treatment earlier this afternoon. I was engrossed in thought." "Oh my god, it talks!" exclaimed Edge, "Apology accepted, English muffin." "My, you're a gracious smart ass, aren't you? Would you like to stop at your local pub for a pint?" Inspector Hunnington asked. "You bet your English ass I would," Edge replied, "I have just the place where you would fit in perfectly." They pulled up the British Pub on Third Street, where a huge flag of Great Britain flew outside on a flagstick—the colors waving in the cold wind of winter. Edge opened the door for the inspector as they entered and looked around the pub. Edge sat down on a chair at the bar, with the inspector next to him. The bartender greeted them with a "Welcome to the British Pub, mates." "What are your pleasures, sirs?" he asked. "Let's have a pint of your best homeland ale, old chap, and one also for my American friend," said the inspector. He looked on as the bartender drew a couple of huge mugs of ale and placed one in front of Edge and the other for the inspector. Edge lifted the mug to his lips, sipped the brew, and held it in his mouth before swallowing hard. "Its warm beer," Edge clamored. He looked at the inspector and said, "Do you like this stuff?" "This is the only way we drink ale in England. Nice and warm," the inspector replied. "Do you think I can get a nice cold beer?" Edge asked the barkeep." "That's why I keep cold beer also, for my American customers," said the barkeep. Edge pushed his warm ale to the inspector, citing he had to have his beer cold. The inspector nodded his approval in agreement. "Warm ale isn't for everyone, Edge," he said. The barkeep started laughing and turned his attention to the soccer game on the telly. This was a nice place with a nice atmosphere. Two televisions were playing different programs at each side of the bar. There were tables in the back of the establishment and booths for people to grab a sandwich and a pint. The inspector tapped the bar with his forefinger, and the barkeep came over. "Do you know where I can get a nice portion of English fish and chips?" the inspector asked. The barkeep looked at him and said, "Yes, we serve that, but our kitchen is closed for the evening, sir. Sorry, mate." "Don't worry about it. I just thought I would inquire about that," Replied the inspector. They finished the pints, got back into the car, and drove to the hotel where the inspector was staying. The inspector exited the vehicle and said to Edge, "I bid you a good evening, Lieutenant Woodredge." Edge turned his head to the inspector, "Warm ale, yeech!" The inspector stood there befuddled, watching as Edge drove away into the night.

Chapter Eighteen

John, aka Jack, had already entered the twenty-first century through the vortex caused by the weather pattern in London. The combination of the rain and wind would produce an eye in the storm, and a vacuum that would draw his carriage through the weather-related vortex. The carriage entered along the Niagara River (upper) on Goat Island, near the point where the view was limited. There were no tourists at this time of night, since the island was closed at dusk, and the only ones on the island were park police. They wouldn't think that anything was unusual about the fog, since it was a common occurrence near the falls. John's carriage sat atop the Goat Island Bridge, stopping to admire the spectacular and mesmerizing sounds of the fast-moving waters. John stepped out from the carriage and strolled to the rail of the bridge, gazing across the way toward the falls, breathing deeply, and taking in the cool night air. His lungs filling with icy capacity of the winter, and his cheeks turned pinkish crimson as the winter breeze whirled through his hair when he had removed his hat. He noticed a movement to his left and observed a cat walking to him. Upon reaching him, it began rubbing its body against his leg, as if asking for his affection. None came. He continued his solace, ignoring the cat, and crossed the road to the other side, changing his view. He was now looking at a more calm view of the river, which he thought was more like him in a way; but so was the other side. He thought to himself, "The two sides of John." He walked to the front of the carriage and patted the horse's mane. Reaching into the inside pocket of his cape, he removed some sugar pellets and let the horses have a treat for their services. Angus sat in his carriage seat with the reins in his hands, wearing black gloves to ward off the cold. He was pleasantly dressed in garb of his time similar to John's, and also was wore a top hat like the one John wore, with the exception that it was not as fancy. He too wore a cape, but it was more weather-beaten than John's. He looked down at John who was still attending to the horses. "Well, my lord, would you druther keep going here or return, since we do not have much time." "We have plenty of time, my friend. Do you think we can stroll the city for another fair maiden?" John asked him. "You've had your fair share here, sir," Angus replied, "You don't want to overstay the welcome, do you, sir?" Angus asked John. "I revel in a challenge, Angus. I like it here—there are many ladies of the evening to choose from in this city. I feel my time and work are almost through here, but the challenge in this is still there." Saying this, John returned to the warmth of his carriage, and as Angus slapped the reins on the horses with a *yaaaaaaa!* shout, the horses responded to his command. The carriage moved along the dark street in its usual slowness.

Inspector Hunnington was still awake, waiting for the weather forecast from Scotland Yard. He was stirring his cup of tea, when the phone in his room alarmed him, since he was deep in thought about the case. It was the evening receptionist at the Yard. "Inspector Hunnington here," he said, just the way he answered all his calls, "Whom am I speaking with, ma'am?" "This is Constable Stephanie Parker, sir. I have the information you requested, sir. It seems that the moon is full tonight, sir. We are encountering a severe thunderstorm, which will probably last all day," came the reply. I see, constable. Thank you for calling me in America, and thank you for the weather report. Will you fax me the remaining reports stat?" he asked. "Yes sir, they are already on the way," Constable Parker responded. "Good evening, Constable, and remind me to spring for tea when I get home." "Good evening, sir, and I will hold you to your word, sir." The conversation had ended, and Inspector Hunnington had to call Lieutenant Woodredge and fill him in on the information he had just received. He pressed Edge's phone number into his phone, and it rang immediately. "This better be good," came the voice on the other end. It was Edge's voice, and he had just gotten to sleep. His voice was raspy from the alcohol and cigarettes. "Who the fuck is this, and what the fuck are you waking me at 3:00 a.m. for?" "It's Inspector Hunnington and . . . . He was cut off by Edge's irritability, "English muffin, what the hell, it's 3:00 a.m." Edge yelled into the phone. "Hush and listen to me, you American asshole. He's here—he's here now!" the inspector exclaimed. Edge sat up on the edge of his bed and listened closely to what the inspector was saying. "I'll pick you up in ten minutes, Inspector. Be ready." "I'll wait out front, Edge," the inspector told him. He grabbed his overcoat and ran toward the door, into the elevator, and out front to wait for Edge. He carefully grabbed his pants and slowly put them on, not to awaken Abbie, since there was no reason for her to come along. She had been traumatized enough. He didn't want to expose her to anymore of John's stares.

Edge rolled up to the front of the Quality Inn, and Inspector Hunnington was waiting for him. He got into the passenger side and explained everything to Edge. "Where do we begin to look for the ripper?" the inspector asked. "I have a gut feeling he will be somewhere near the falls. If not, then we drive around until we see an unusual fog-like appearance in the city. We will check out the areas the hookers frequent most. The RAC patrol has many of them locked up in our holding center, but we can't hold them too long," Edge said to him. Edge drove to Goat Island, stopped at the barrier, lifted it, continued over the bridge onto the island, and then stopped suddenly. He had noticed carriage tracks in the snow. Turning around, he started to follow the tracks slowly, down Buffalo Avenue, to Tenth Street, to Fall Street, and straight to Niagara Street. It was snowing lightly, and they were hoping the snow wouldn't cover the tracks made by the carriage. The tracks were fading as the snow was masking John's trek to find another victim—farther down Niagara Street, to Portage Road, and then again to Niagara Street. After turning onto Niagara Street, they noticed a strange fog-like appearance ahead of them. "That has to be him in that fog, Edge," the inspector said. "I agree wholeheartedly, Inspector," Edge came back. Edge's car sped and pulled up in front of the fog. The fog seemed to stop in front of them. They could barely make out the carriage. Edge and the inspector exited Edge's car with weapons drawn. Edge had a 9 mm automatic, and the inspector a 38-caliber six-shooter. They were both at the fog. Angus had stopped the carriage horses just before to avoid hitting the vehicle. The horses shied and bolted at the sight of the skidding car. The two could hear the horses snort and stomp their hooves in the snow. "Get out of the fucking carriage, now," Edge demanded. John stepped out of the carriage and appeared before them. "I bid you a wonderful morning. What is the meaning of this exhibition? You are blocking my way," John said to them. "I am Lieutenant Woodredge, Niagara Falls Police, and this is Inspector Hunnington of Scotland Yard. Who the fuck are you?" said Edge, commanding an answer. "My name is John, and this is my driver Angus. You can lower your weapons—I mean you no harm," John told them. "No can do, Johnny boy! The guns stay pointed at you," the inspector said sternly. "Well, suit yourself, Inspector, and I must say that I am impressed with Scotland Yard being present," John smiled at them. "You're under suspicion of murder and illegal entry into the United States. You both are coming with us for questioning," Inspector Hunnington said. "I beg to differ, sir, since I need to get to work, and you are preventing me from doing so. I think it is time for me to bid you a pleasant day. Inspector, you are a noble man, but the American is an imbecile. Have a pleasant day, gentlemen," John told them as he entered once again into the carriage. Gun shots rang from Edge's 9 mm, while the inspector didn't fire any. Edge fired blindly into the fog, hitting the carriage twice and Angus once in the lower leg. The other shot missed everything. As the firing was going on, a lightning bolt hit the top of the carriage where the crown ornament and the point sticking from its top sat, and the carriage was gone in a flash, leaving the inspector and Edge stupefied. They both lowered their weapons and looked at each other, bewildered. They both got back into their vehicle and were speechless all the way back to the inspector's hotel. Edge broke the silence, "That was one hundred percent fucking freaky." He was looking at the inspector now. The inspector returned the look, and it was a puzzling look. "I can't agree more, mate," he said. "Why did you shoot?" the inspector asked. "They were fleeing from murder charges," Edge explained. "I know I hit one of them—I think I shot the driver," he continued. "Where the other bullets went, I don't know. Hopefully into John. We almost had him, Inspector," Edge said solemnly. "It's almost daylight, Edge. What do you say we call it a night, or morning?" the inspector replied. "I say I'm ready for a twelve-pack," Edge turned and smiled. The inspector stepped out of the vehicle and entered the hotel. Walking past Stacey who was swabbing the lobby floor, he turned and asked her what time tea was. Her look was that of amazement, since she was not up-to-date on English customs. "Breakfast?" he asked again. "The kitchen will open at 7 a.m., sir, but the coffee is already made here in the lobby," she smiled at him, continuing to mop the floor. He walked to the coffeemaker and poured a cup. Then, taking out a bottle of scotch from his pocket—a small bottle at that—he tipped part of its contents into his coffee. He left the lobby area to the elevator to his room. What an ordeal, this morning—what an ordeal," he pondered.

Edge returned to his apartment with his twelve-pack, unlocked the door, and noticed Abbie was still sleeping, though stirring a bit. He sat on the side of the bed and cracked open a cold Coors Light. Abbie heard the opening of the can and looked over her shoulder, half asleep. "What's with the beer, babe?" she asked. "We almost had him, pumpkin," he replied. "Had who?" another question. "I mean, I heard you yelling into the phone, but I thought it was a crank call. Who did you almost have?" "We almost had Jack the Ripper. I think I shot his driver. I fired four shots into the fog, and I heard a sharp cry." Her eyes grew wide with excitement and her sleepiness subsided. She wanted to hear everything that happened, and Edge proceeded to go over every detail, beginning with why he didn't wake her and bring her along as backup. She understood his worries and was not angry at him at all. He was only protecting her—she could relate to that. She wrapped her arms around his neck as she listened tentatively, kissing the nape of his neck to help him relax. He didn't respond to her kissing since he couldn't believe what he had witnessed this morning. Something was bothering him about the whole scenario. He would try to sleep and get together with the inspector later. Edge finished his story as Abbie listened closely, now sitting next to him on the bed. He had finished his third beer by now, and his adrenalin was slowing his body's metabolism to a degree of crashing. He laid his head on the pillow, and Abbie laid her head in the crutch of his shoulder as he drifted off to dreamland. Her eyes remained open and on guard as thoughts ran through her brain. She needed to protect him as he slept. Jack the Ripper would not come by this a.m.

Chapter Nineteen

Angus's leg was a bloody pulp of splintered bone fragments and pieces of wood as Edge's bullet had caught a piece of the carriage's baseboard at the driver's foot. Angus looked down and began picking the wood from his wound. Each piece removed eased some of the pain, but the wound was still throbbing. He then wrapped his kerchief around the area and tied a tight knot. Gimping down from the driver's mount, he opened the door for John (Jack) to step out, who knew something was wrong, since it took too long for Angus to get to the door. Angus looked at John and then down at the cobblestone street. "The goomer shot me in my bloody leg, me lord," Angus told him. "Well, get to the health clinic, my dear friend, and I will take care of all expenses," John said. "It seems they were on to us, me lord. Were they?" "I'm not sure, Angus, but that one constable doesn't hesitate to fire that weapon. Does he?" John smiled. "No! I can attest to that, sir," said Angus as he grimaced in pain as his lower leg throbbed uncontrollably. "I will be speaking to you later. I think I'll stroll a little before I bid the evening adieu. Now you get going and attend to your wound before an infection sets in. Then take care of the horses and carriage. I'll see you at the mansion. Good-night and Godspeed, Angus." John left Angus as he began strolling down the street, looking for his next victim. "Good-night, sir, and thank you, sir," Angus replied as he climbed painfully back aboard the carriage for the trip to the clinic.

Edge was still sleeping while Abbie had been up awhile drinking a cup of coffee, watching him move around the bed restlessly. She had listened of the experience in the early morning hours he had had with the inspector. In a way, she was glad she was not there. She saw John's eyes, looked into them, and knew what she had seen was pure evil. Something about him was evil. Could it be his movements? Was it his voice? Was it his demeanor as a gentleman? Or the surrounding element? No! It was the eyes. There was something about his eyes—hypnotic and soulless. There was no soul behind those eyes—just evil. Evil, evil eyes. She would never forget what she saw in them as they stared into her, piercing her inner soul. It was a feeling she couldn't shake. She was surprised she didn't have nightmares about the eyes attacking her.

The phone rang in Edge's apartment, and Abbie rose to answer it before it woke Edge. It was Captain Eckersley on the other end, wondering if they were still on the city's payroll as police officers or if they were on a sabbatical. "Edge had a busy evening, sir. We'll be in in a couple of hours," she said. "Report to my office as soon as you three get your clothes on," he said, insinuating that Inspector Hunnington had spent the night and they had a threesome. "Very well, sir. Will do," she replied, hanging the receiver back on the cradle. Edge stirred a bit, opened his eyes a crack to let in some light, closed them again, and grunted a morning, or rather, afternoon grunt. "What time is it, love," Edge asked her. "It's four thirty in the afternoon, and the captain already called," she responded. "Oh shit!" he cried out. "I gotta get a freaking shower. I smell of beer and bullshit." "Yea, I know, I can tell, you smelly ass slob. I'll get you some coffee while you get your stinking ass in the shower," she said, laughing at him. "All right, smart ass, I'll see you in a few," he retorted, heading to the shower while removing his clothes as he went.

She could hear him in the shower, singing dirty songs he had heard at a John Valby concert, and that was one pet peeve of hers—she hated to hear that badly toned, beer-rasping voice singing. He could not carry a note. She wasn't about to tell him that for he was too macho for any woman to try to explain to him about his bad habits, especially his singing. She had his coffee poured as he walked out of the bathroom totally nude, toweling off. As he dropped the towel on the floor—where everything went—she handed him the coffee. He sipped it, set it down on the table, and looked at Abbie as she glanced at his enlargement. "How about a quickie," he said. "We have to get to the station. The captain wants to talk to us. I think the chief's riding his ass about the ripper killings." "Fuck the chief and fuck the captain. I need the time of day here," he said with half a puppy look on his face. "All right, Edge, I'll give you a quickie. She walked to the sink, filled a glass of cold water, walked back to Edge, and poured it all over his manhood. He jumped back in surprise as the cold water hit the bull's-eye, causing goose bumps to run up and down his legs. "What the hell, Abbie," he cried with a stunned look on his face. "There's your quickie, my darling," she said smiling. Edge grabbed the towel from the floor, dried the area off, picked up his drawers, and put them on. After they finished dressing, they had to pick up the inspector at the hotel.

Edge was still irritated with Abbie about the quickie he had just gotten and that he had not been fulfilled. "Those are the breaks, I guess, when you're in love," he thought, "silly ass jokes." When they arrived at Quality Inn, the inspector was ready and waiting. Entering the vehicle, the inspector gave them both his English greeting, Edge just mumbled something under his breath without appreciation, and Abbie gave a smiley "good afternoon". The ride was a quiet one as no one really wanted to speak about the morning before. Edge needed a beer, and the inspector already had his tasty choice hidden inside his jacket pocket—scotch whiskey. Abbie was neutral. She had already had coffee and a quickie, and she was ready for the day. They had taken the scenic route to the station house because Edge had to get smokes and a paper. Edge stopped at B&B on Main Street, grabbed what he needed, and also picked up a few scratchies for Abbie to do on the way. If he didn't pick them up for her, he would have never heard the end of it, until she aggravated him beyond his ability to control himself. So, he thought of her, and she appreciated it by throwing cold water on his pee-pee. "So be it, or so be it not," he thought, "Women are so unpredictable at times." He didn't think she would ever throw cold water on him, knowing his temper the way it is. He figured she would "drop Jones" on him, and he would be set—in a lot better mood than he was in now, not that he was in a bad, bad mood, just slightly irritated.

They finally made it to the station, and as they entered the near-empty squad room, the captain was pushing his pencil or pen. As the pencil-pushing went, the trio knocked and then opened the door. The captain looked up, motioning the three to have a seat. He then continued writing his quarterly report, which he handed to the chief each of the four quarters of the year. This was the last quarter of this year, and the captain wanted to give the chief a final disposition on the ripper case. "What have you three to tell me about the ripper case? Any more leads? Dead bodies? Evidence? Speak to me people? I need something to give the chief," his voice was mellow as none of them had ever heard, like when you have hemorrhoids and they're really inflamed. Edge started to tell the captain about their ordeal with John (Jack), but was cut off by the inspector. "We almost had him?" the captain asked in a questionable tone. He looked quizzically at them and went back to his report. "What happened to him?" he asked. The inspector looked at Edge and looked back. "Go ahead, muffin. You opened your piehole—now it's your show," said Edge as he slouched further into the chair. The captain was getting irritated with him. "No! Inspector, it's not your show," he said, slamming his hand down on the papers in front of him, causing a slight achiness in his palm. "Edge, you tell me what went on!" he commanded, his tone darkening, "You're the lead detective on this case." Edge began to tell the captain how the inspector received a phone call from London, and how he phoned him at 3:00 a.m. and they tracked the fog apparition to Niagara Street, where they fishtailed the car to stop in front of it, with weapons drawn. How they barely made out the carriage, and how John (Jack) spoke to them. This piqued the captain's interest, and his irritability subsided. Edge got to the part where he fired four shots in the carriage's direction, and the captain's eyes went wide as silver dollars. He didn't need the IAD (Internal Affairs Division) in on this case also. Edge finally told him how the carriage was hit by a bolt of lightning and it disappeared. The captain looked bewildered. "It just disappeared, huh?" the captain wondered aloud, "What is this? The X-files? Carriages don't just disappear into thin air." "No, Cap'n, a bolt of lightning caused it to disappear," Edge told him, and the inspector nodded his head in a yes motion. Abbie just sat there listening. She had no input as she was not there to confirm their story. "There was nothing we could do about it, skipper," Edge said. "I guess I can't fault you guys—you're doing a great job. Now tell me how he gets here?" the captain asked. The inspector looked at Edge and told the captain about his theory of moon phases and weather patterns. The captain looked astonished. "Here we go again with the X-files stuff. Now the question is, how do we stop him? We have to prevent him from coming here if he travels by lightning, or whatever. OK people, I'll inform the chief on the progress of the investigation, and you get to work on theories you have to stop him from coming here. We don't need any more dead women turning up on our streets. Dismissed. Keep me posted." As they were all leaving, the captain pulled Edge aside. "The chief said do whatever it takes to solve this case, OK Edge? He needs the mayor to get out of his ass," Captain Eckersley stated. "If he bleeds, I can kill him," Edge replied.

The inspector and Abbie were busy bees at the conference table, again calculating John's next move. Little did they know it would not come for some time. It could be weeks or even months before he would maybe make his next appearance. They knew he was not scared off by Edge's bullets. She knew John wouldn't scare that easily. They would keep their senses and options open, for when he decided to make himself known again, they were to be ready.

Edge on the other hand had his own plans, and his first plan was to get a beer. He stopped at the British Pub for cold English ale as he had told the barkeep the last time to keep one ice for him. He sat at the barstool and hammered away at the ice-cold ale. He ordered a second, and that one went down smoother than the first. He bid the barkeep a good day in his own way—usually sarcastic of course—and left. He needed those ales after meeting with the captain—which was usually the case—'cause the skipper could be unbearable. His second plan of action was to bait John again, but on the other hand he didn't want anyone's death on his conscience—not that he cared whether they lived or died, but just to avoid any finger-pointing his way. Edge had an "I don't give a shit" attitude when it came to suspects or persons of interest. He did what it took to get the job done. He had his way, and the law had its own. Either way, his arrest record could not be tarnished. The guy in the trunk was one of the lucky ones—he got off easy. The broken nose would be a reminder of his drinking problem. Edge would perhaps see him again if he decided to complain about it. The next time it would be jail time. He wasn't worried about it, though, since the guy probably realized he was wrong for trying to skip out on the bill.

Edge sat in his assigned vehicle with the heater running, clanging as it may—the noise getting on his nerves and very little warmth coming from the vents. He thought what a piece of shit this car was and the city should spring for new ones. He knew that wasn't going to happen since the city was crying aloud for more federal funds. Or state funds. Forget about jobs. Forget the people. Keep the politicians' pockets lined. Raise the friggin' taxes. People move out. Freeloaders move in. Beggars abound. He puts one crackhead in jail, and two more are made. If they let him have his way, the crackheads would do it cold turkey, in a vacant room, filth all over the floor. There were many vacant properties he could secure and get these scum suckers off the street. He would lock them in a room with no windows and watch them scurry around like a wounded animal. He would give them water, but very little food. They needed their confidence back again. No, he was just cruel like that, to watch them writhe in discomfort—like going to a sporting event and rooting for the home team. He was sick in this aspect as being a police officer or a person for which needed to be taught a valuable lesson in life. He would sit there and watch, enjoying their pain and getting much pleasure from it, or maybe even masturbating while he is watching. Unfortunately he didn't have the time for this, and he just arrested them and threw their worthless asses in jail. The fantasy was nice a one though.

The clanging in the heater lessened a bit, and he pulled away from the curb around the corner to St. Peter's Episcopal Church. He had an appointment with the pastor, whose name was Rev. Robert Townsend. Edge had known Rev. Townsend since he was a kid. He had been a good advisor on many subjects, guiding Edge when he had problems. He was a stout man, short in stature, with balding in the back and white hair on the sides of his head. He has a slight lisp when he spoke, and that was constantly. Sometimes Edge had to shut him up because he constantly egged Edge on about why he didn't come to church. That day, Edge needed his authoritative professional help. Edge opened the door to his rectory office, and the pastor was on the phone, motioning Edge to sit. He looked around the room with all the pictures of Jesus and the Blessed Virgin Mary. The pastor's desk was solid oak and neatly polished, and the top was neatly arranged. Many religious books were neatly kept on his bookshelves. Many crosses were hanging from the walls, and he had a large one with a figure of the Christ attached to a wooden cross above is head where he sat. Edge couldn't help but to contemplate what would happen if the cross ever fell off the wall. It would kill him instantly, since it appeared to be that heavy. What a way to go—Death by Christ. Perhaps it would be an appropriate way to go—being an apostle of God. Edge just sat there and grinned, listening to the conversation between the pastor and the party on the other end. It was a one-sided listening experience. Rev. Townsend held up one finger so as to tell Edge that he would take one more minute, which turned into ten minutes.

After hanging the receiver on the cradle, the reverend gave Edge his total attention. The Rev looked at Edge and held out both hands. "I'm all yours, Lieutenant Woodredge. What am I able to do for you? You sounded a little worried over the phone when you called me. Is there a problem in your personal life?" he asked. "No, I have a case that may need your expertise. It has to do with the dead hookers. Actually it may be about, maybe something a little supernatural. I'm having trouble believing it myself. I wouldn't have believed it if I didn't see it for myself," Edge continued to tell Rev. Townsend about everything pertaining to the case, and his thoughts about how to catch the ripper. "What's your religious take on this case?" Edge asked him. This might have been the first time the reverend was speechless. He sat there with his forefinger resting on the side his face, and his chin resting on his thumb and the palm of his hand. The reverend looked grimly at Edge and then spoke slowly and eloquently so Edge could connect with what he was saying. "It sounds like you need to exorcise the demon to remain in his own century," he said. "You will need a priest who specializes in exorcisms to perform a special exorcism to keep this demon in his own century," he went on. "What about you, Rev?" Edge asked. "Well, yea, I could do it, but I would need the church's permission, and that could take months to get," he explained to him. "I don't have months or weeks. I have maybe a few days at that," Edge told him. "Let me work on the church part of it, and I'll get back to you on that," Rev. Townsend said. "Thank you for time, Rev, and I'll be waiting for your call."

The reverend sounded promising on the exorcism idea, and Edge hopped in his car and decided to fill in the inspector and Abbie on this idea of an exorcism. Edge didn't believe in all this hocus-pocus exorcism crap, but if it worked, they would be rid of John (Jack the Ripper) hopefully for good. Edge went to his apartment, ran up the stairs, opened the door, and went in and grabbed a beer bottle. He rinsed it out, put the twist-off bottle cap back on, and ran out the door and back in his car to the police headquarters; but he had to make a stop first.

Edge pulled up to St. Joseph's Church on Pine Avenue and ran up the stairs to the entrance way of the church. He untwisted the cap and dipped the beer bottle in the bowl of holy water. Leaving a donation in the flower donation box, Edge left as his car was still running to keep it warm. He was then on his way to the station house, driving down Pine Avenue to Hyde Park Boulevard. Edge turned right onto the boulevard, into the parking area.

The inspector and Abbie agreed that John (Jack) would be entering this century again in a couple of days. Edge walked in with his beer bottle in hand as they were leaving the conference room. "Do you think this is a good time to drink beer, Edge?" Abbie asked. "It's not beer, but now that you asked, yes, it is a good time to drink beer," he smiled at her. "Don't let the captain see you with that, or you'll be standing tall in front of him," she pointed out. Meanwhile, the inspector was curious and was looking at the beer bottle filled with holy water. "This is holy water in the bottle," Edge shot back. "Who in their right mind would put holy water in a beer bottle?" But she answered her own question because Edge wasn't in his right mind three-quarters of the time anyway. "Come on in the conference room, and I'll tell you all about my theory," Edge entered the room, followed by the duo, and they sat down to listen to Edge's madness.

Chapter Twenty

Rev. Robert Townsend left Niagara Falls for a meeting with the Honorable Bishop Royal McNulty in the Buffalo diocese of the Episcopal Church about the possibility of himself doing an exorcism. It was his call. The bishop's office was located at the St. Paul's Cathedral—the diocese of Western New York. It was a well-built church with tall steeples and excellent architecture. Colorful stained glass marked all the windows. Many articulate columns were present in the main sanctuary. The pews were made of beautifully carved wood. The organ was spacious, and the pipes were huge in nature. Rev. Townsend was waiting outside in the rectory hall to be called by the bishop's assistant. The bishop was a busy man, not only providing services for his own parish and congregation, but also fulfilling duties that included all of Western New York's episcopal churches.

Rev. Townsend had phoned the bishop earlier in the day to request an audience of the utmost importance so he could dutifully explain the problem the Niagara Falls Police were having with these murders. He had told the bishop it was a matter of life and death, which, in a way, it was. He had brought the prayer book with him, and the writ of exorcism also. He was sitting there thinking about his presentation to the bishop because he had to make a good impression to His Eminence. He had to make it believable. He also knew the bishop took a hard stance on this type of religious order. It would or might take a great deal of convincing on his part to make the bishop see things his way. Maybe he should have brought Lieutenant Woodredge with him to help, but then again Lieutenant Woodredge would have probably gotten out of hand and lost his temper. As the reverend sat there admiring the gold-inlaid borders on the walls and the many paintings hanging in the hall, he was having second thoughts about his audience with the bishop. Most ministers thought of the bishop as a boss, but he was hoping the bishop would welcome him as a friend. He stood and walked a bit, as nervous as a patient waiting to see the doctor for the first time.

Finally a soft voice came from the hallway door, "The bishop will see you now, Rev. Townsend," as the assistant motioned him to enter. "Thank you, my child," said Rev. Townsend as he entered through her office door and then to the bishop's office. The bishop was standing behind his desk with his right hand extended, palm down. The reverend clasped his hand as in a handshake gesture, and gently bent down and kissed his insignia ring. "Good afternoon, Your Excellency, and thank you for this audience," he said as he gently let go of his hand. "Your servant, Rev. Townsend. Please sit down. Now what is so urgent that you seek my assistance," Bishop McNulty said, smiling at him. Rev. Townsend looked at the floor, thought he would just get it over with, and blurted out, "I need to perform an exorcism." He continued to explain to the bishop the reasoning for the exorcism—that the police needed the church's help in solving the murders of the prostitutes. The bishop sat there, unmoving in his chair, with total attention to what the reverend was telling him. The exorcism would be a tall order. He knew this, but he blurted out everything anyway, and the bishop sat there silently with an unbelieving stare in his eyes. The bishop hadn't heard anything this absurd in a very long time. An exorcism in the twenty-first century was unheard of in America, and to have an Episcopalian minister perform it was next to impossible. This was securely for the Catholic faith.

Bishop McNulty just sat there glancing at Rev. Townsend and then at Christ's cross on the wall, as if to ask for his guidance. The reverend just sat there with his hands folded with one another in silence. He stared at the floor, waiting for a reply from the bishop. "You know, Rev. Townsend, exorcisms aren't done anymore, at least not in the United States anyway. Maybe in impoverished countries, but not here. I'll tell you what I'm going to do. If you provide me with the case files, I'll review them, and we'll meet again, and I'll give you my decision then." "Agreed," the bishop said. "All I can ask of you, Your Eminence, is your fair and righteous decision," said the reverend, rising from his chair, kissing the bishop's ring again, and then exiting the office to ask Lieutenant Woodredge for the case files.

Edge was leaning back on his chair at his desk, waiting for the call from the good reverend, which would never come, since the reverend was himself on his way to see Edge. If need be, Edge would contact the Catholic priest at St. Joe's on Pine Avenue. This would have been a better choice, since the Catholics were better acquainted with this ritual. Rev. Townsend was a long-time friend of Edge's since he was a child. Maybe he should have gone along for support, but then again, Edge knew he couldn't keep his sarcastic mouth shut. Edge had faith in the good reverend to get the job done. He could talk and talk, and could probably talk the pope into becoming protestant. He would talk to Edge for hours on end, especially when Edge was being investigated for the shooting of Ace on Highland Avenue. He would talk about various subjects, but when it came to the church and going to the services, Edge drew the line and changed the subject. Edge wasn't interested in this type of chatter.

The reverend walked into the station house and straight for Edge's desk. Edge was deep in thought, and the reverend's appearance startled him; he almost fell out of his chair onto the floor. "What gives, Reverend? You scared the bejesus out of me. What's the answer—yes or no—on the exorcism? Don't hold back on me now," Edge was razzing him. "His Eminence would like a copy of the case files so it can give him a guideline for his decision," Rev. Townsend said. "All right, Rev, I'll get the files to you as soon as Detective Cook in the conference room gets done flirting with the English muffin," Edge said, half smiling. "Very well, Lieutenant, I will expect them whenever," Rev. Townsend stared at Edge. "Is there something else I can do for you, Reverend?" Edge asked. "Yes, Lieutenant, there is, but you won't like what I'm going to ask—when are you going to come to church?" Rev. Townsend said with a broad smile. "When hell freezes over, sir, when hell freezes over," said Edge as he got up, gave the minister a hug, and entered the conference room. Rev. Townsend was left stymied by what Edge said to him. He thought to himself, even if Edge did go to church, the church might not survive Edge. The reverend left to return to his parish.

"Abbie, I need a copy of the case files for Rev. Townsend to present to the bishop. Also, I need a copy of the weather report from you, Inspector Bloke, '*stat*' like yesterday, OK muffin tea cake?" Edge commanded. "Edge, why do you have to be so obnoxious all the time?" Abbie scolded him. "Because I'm tired of this John dude and all the nonsense that is associated with him. So far he's ahead of us, and he knows it. I want to get him before he strikes again," Edge said with a slight tilt of his head. "Well, we all want to get him, especially me. Don't be hard on the inspector—he's here to help. With his expertise and knowledge on Jack the Ripper, his volubility is golden. I think you should apologize to him for those remarks," Abbie waved her hand at him. "As I told the reverend, I'm telling you—when hell freezes over. I need a beer," Edge turned and left.

The inspector was in the captain's office as Edge was leaving the conference room. Edge looked over at the captain and noticed him motioning for him to come in his office. Edge had a feeling the muffin was ratting him out for calling him names. Edge was wondering why the inspector left the room in a hurry. Edge entered the skipper's office and was told to take a seat. Edge sat slouched in the chair, which was his normal posture. "What's up, skipper?" Edge asked. "I'm not happy with the way you've been treating Inspector Hunnington. We have certain protocol here when we have guest officers from another country. The inspector from now on will be treated with the utmost respect. He's not a cheeky fellow or a bloody bloke or anything pertaining to his nationality. No more pet names. Ya got me, Lieutenant?" the captain said sternly. "Gotcha,

Capt'n," Edge said smiling. "You're dismissed, Lieutenant. Get the hell out of here," the captain said, glaring at him.

The two of them left the office, and Edge burst out laughing for the whole squad room to hear. Everyone looked up, and they knew the lieutenant had just got his ass reamed by the captain. They all knew that Edge didn't care one way or the other. The inspector looked baffled at Edge's behavior and returned to the conference room. Edge continued his laughter until the inspector was out of earshot. "He's a big English candy-ass," Edge said, causing the rest of the room to join in his laughter. Edge popped his head into the room and told Abbie and the inspector it was getting late, and that they should call it a night. He felt nothing was going to happen since his shooting at the carriage. The captain agreed it was time to go, and motioned to the trio to leave. The captain was on his way out, when Edge yelled to him, "Hey Capt'n, what do ya say we stop at the British Pub for a quick pint of ale?" The skipper got into his car and the trio got into Edge's, and they all headed to the British Pub. They arrived with the captain in tow, strolled to the bar, and had a seat. Edge ordered his usual and three ales for the others. The captain sipped his ale and a spray came from his lips all over the bar as the ale was warm. A slight drip was coming from the captain's mouth as he began to wipe it off with a napkin. "What the hell!" the captain said with the ale all over his suit and overcoat. Edge was laughing, and the inspector joined in also. "A bit too strong for ya, is it, Captain?" the inspector inquired. Abbie just looked over, stunned at what the captain did. "Did I miss something?" Abbie asked. "It's what you didn't miss, Detective," the captain said, "This ale is fucking warm." "I think you just received a bit of English custom, Captain," the inspector said. Edge ordered the barkeep to give the captain and Abbie a cold beer after the joke ended. Edge looked at the captain, and the captain returned a cold stare.

"You had your fun, Lieutenant. I'll admit you got me on that one. You owe me a dry cleaning, smart ass," the captain said in his direction. "It takes a little getting used to," the inspector looked at him, smiling, "That was a nasty joke, but a good one." "Paybacks are definitely a bitch in order for you, Lieutenant," Captain Eckersley was now smiling. The captain finished his beer, stood and bid the trio a good evening, and left for the night. A few minutes later, the inspector rose from the barstool and told them, "I think I will walk about your downtown area before I retire for the evening." He nodded to Edge and tipped his hat to Abbie as he left the pub. Edge looked at Abbie with a puppy dog look on his face. "Well, my darling, do you feel like getting lucky?" he asked. "Me get lucky! I think it's the other way around, buster," she said with a sudden surprise to her voice.

Edge and Abbie left the pub, leaving Edge's car in front as it was a brief walk to Edge's apartment. As they entered the darkened apartment, Edge threw Abbie on the bed and began kissing her passionately about the neck and between her breasts. Her hands were around his neck, and she returned his kiss in kind. He was a horn-dog, and she sensed his feelings as he was on top of her. "Hold on," she said, "I have to catch my breath—it was a long way up those stairs, buddy boy." He rolled over, sat up, and removed his coat and shoes. She did the same. Abbie stood and straddled Edge as he was sitting on the side of the bed. Her arms draped around his neck and her legs wrapped around his waist, she gave him a long-drawn kiss. She could feel a sudden rise in him, and smiled. "Seems like someone else just woke up, sweetie," she said. "Uh, huh," was his reply as he was removing her shirt and bra. He tossed them aside and rolled her over on her back, kissing her passionately on the neck and breasts, down to her naval. As he undid the belt on her slacks and pulled down the zipper, the pants were soon off. She lay there in just her panties. "How about a rain check, love?" she asked. Edge looked at her and with a tilt of his head said, "You've got to be kidding me, woman? Look at me," as he stood and she gazed at the bulge in his pants. "What do you suppose we are going to do about this?" he was pointing in the direction of his groin. "I'm sorry, my dear, but women have this certain problem every month that we can't control," she told him. "Well, how about working on your dental degree, baby?" said Edge, standing in front of her, smiling—his crotch right at her face. She grabbed hold of his manhood through his trousers and squeezed slightly. "How about I put my gun to his head and end his misery?" she stood with his crotch in hand and lightly pecked him on the lips. She began to walk to the bathroom, turned around, removed her panties, held them out in front of her, and let them drop to the floor. Standing in front of him butt-naked, she swiveled her hips slightly, and turned and entered the bathroom. Edge, standing facing the bathroom, yelled to her, "You're a dick tease."

Abbie entered the shower and began washing her hair, thinking she should have succumbed to Edge's advances. She knew he was like a big baby, and she didn't feel much like babysitting tonight. She finished her shower and dried off. Then wrapping the towel around her, she opened the door and stepped into the empty room. Edge had left. She figured he was pissed off, and went to grab a six-pack and drink his horniness away. He probably went to the point and would sit half the night thinking and drinking. It was his place where he could have peace and quiet. It was a serene place. The only noise he would hear was the roaring thunder of the falls. Abbie lay on the bed, and as soon as her head hit the pillow, dreamland began.

Chapter Twenty-One

Edge didn't go to the point tonight; instead he sat on a bench on Third Street and lit a ciggy. He didn't feel much like a beer anymore. He wanted a little peace and quiet, except for the traffic on the street. It wasn't going to be so this evening, since on a bench across the street was a couple having a spat. It seemed to be a one-way disagreement, with a young fella yelling at the lady sitting on the bench he could only presume was his girlfriend. Edge kept glancing at them, and she was crying uncontrollably. He kept on yelling—more like screaming—at her, and it was getting to be annoying to Edge. He was thinking about when John would strike next and how Abbie turned him down, one thought after the next. The twosome kept getting louder, she continued to cry, and Edge kept getting more annoyed. Edge continued to stare at the fella doing the yelling, and it finally dawned on him that he was being watched. Edge wasn't exactly dressed like a cop, and he hadn't shaved in days, so this fella figured maybe Edge was a bum out for a few nickels so he could buy a bottle of wine or whatever he preferred. The young fella kept looking at Edge as Edge stared back. "Hey dude, do you want something? Gotta a nose problem? Mind your business, buster. This is between me and her. Ain't got nuttin' to do with you, so look somewhere else," the fella said with a stern voice.

Edge looked away, and then got up and walked over to the fella. "Leave the lady alone, and I won't say it again," Edge commanded. The fella grabbed his girlfriend's cheeks of her face with one hand, and Edge grabbed the nape of his neck; the punch landed square on the fella's front teeth. The fella never saw it coming. He began to spit out teeth onto the street. He grasped his mouth in pain. He tried to swing at Edge, who avoided the blow and tripped the fella, landing him on the seat of his pants. He sat there, holding his mouth with a puzzled look on his face. "Stay down, mister. If you get up, you'll regret it. Now take some sound advice and treat this lady like she should be treated. No more abuse, verbal or otherwise," Edge's tone was authoritative. The man grabbed his cell phone and began to call 911. "Don't bother with the police; one just gave you an ass-beating," said Edge as he took the cell phone away from him and gave it to his girlfriend. "Are you all right?" Edge asked her, and she shook her head to say yes. "I live right across the street in apartment three, and if he continues this behavior toward you, come and get me." She nodded yes. The fella got up from the sidewalk, brushing his pants free from snow, and walked away with his girlfriend in tow. He continuously looked back to see if Edge was following.

Edge walked back to his bench and lit up another ciggy. He sat in peace for a while. The cigarette seemed to taste better after he gave ass-beatings, or maybe it was adrenalin rushing through him. No, he thought, it always tasted better after he gave a beating. He sat there smiling, as was his nature after he gave a beating, He seemed to enjoy it. That dude had it coming anyway. Even if he didn't, he would have gotten one anyway, be it Edge who did it or someone else. The lady didn't deserve to be treated like that. Edge didn't think he would treat her like that again, after missing a few teeth. Edge looked at his knuckles; the son of a bitch had cut his middle knuckle. He figured his tooth must have cut it, but Edge didn't care. The guy got what was coming to him.

Edge sat there in the chilly night air, looking up and down Third Street, monitoring the flow of traffic and watching as the drunks staggered out of the bars to their cars. "How stupid," he thought, "If I was a patrolman, I could have so many DUI's, I would be the king of the department. Edge—king of the DUI's. That would be me." As Edge began to nightdream while he was awake, he thought he was having a bad dream, when he looked down the street and noticed the inspector walking toward him. Inspector Hunnington reached Edge, and acknowledging him said, "Good evening again, Lieutenant Woodredge. Not so lucky I see." "Meaning what?" Edge responded. "Meaning with your lady friend," he replied. "Hey, ya got me on that one, Inspector. Got shut out tonight," said Edge, looking sad since he didn't get his own way. "So, why are you out so late tonight?" he asked the inspector. "I have been strolling about, thinking about our mutual friend we're after. I was contemplating capturing him. You know, set a trap, capture him, and then try him on capital murders. It would be nice to see him fry like a blooming onion. Wouldn't it, Sledge?" the inspector asked. "*Aaarg*," was Edge's reply. He hated being called Sledge. It sounded like a hammer. "First of all, English muffin, my name is Edge, and second of all, New York doesn't have a death penalty." "I see that we have a predicament," the inspector stated. He looked at Edge's hand and noticed he was bleeding. "What do we have here?" he asked, pointing to the wound on Edge's knuckle. "I had to teach a guy some etiquette of treating a lady," Edge responded. "Isn't that a bit of police brutality? You should have arrested him," the inspector pondered. "Hey, he swung at me second, so I just gave him what his momma should have given him a long time ago," Edge smiled. Ass-beating 101 was what Edge taught tonight.

Inspector Hunnington smiled at Edge and bid him a good evening. He continued on down Third Street until he was out of sight. Edge was relieved to see the inspector had left him alone to his solitude of himself and his thoughts.

His thoughts were of Abbie, who was still haunted by the events of John's (Jack's) actions upon her. She had had many nightmares since her ordeal. Tonight she seemed to be sleeping peacefully with a little help from a sleep aid the doctor prescribed for her. Edge called it her antipsychotic drug that would send her into her woman's mood where she would give him the look and then not speak to him for three days. He would laugh at her for this, and that would infuriate her even more. Edge loved to tease the hell out of her. He could get her going better than anyone at the department. Of course, Edge could get the pope angry if he put his mind and mouth to it. The captain couldn't control Edge; he called Edge a loose cannon—a psycho with a badge and a gun. Edge figured that people just misjudged him. He thought he got the job done, and that's all that mattered.

It was getting colder outside, and Edge decided to walk the downtown area before heading back home. He got up and headed east on Third Street, past the bars that were beginning to close for the evening. He walked past Bank of America, where he noticed two patrols' cars parked with their windows down, their occupants conversing with one another. He ignored the both of them, not even acknowledging their existence with a wave of his hand. They beeped their horns at him, but he didn't even look in their direction. He kept right on walking, crossing Rainbow Boulevard, past the Seneca office building, to the stairs to the casino. He stood at the top of the stairs, breathing in the cold night air. His mood had lessened, and a slight depression set in. He needed some more action to get his body pumping and adrenalin flowing again. Maybe he could find it at the casino. Maybe he could catch a cheater or a thief trying to better his odds to beat the house. Even though the casino had its own Seneca Marshall, he would love to assist.

Edge entered the casino with his badge showing, and he could hear the security guard radio to other guards that there was a police officer in the house. He wandered through the slot area where most of the rip-offs took place. People were depositing nickels and quarters in various machines. Double diamonds was a favorite. There was a slot machine for just about every game show on television—even old shows. The casino was pretty lively even in the middle of the night. The blackjack tables seemed to be full. The casino was as busy as usual, and Edge kept a keen eye on everyone, especially the old ladies, since they could be easily distracted by any scam artist or artists working together. The biggest scam was the distraction scheme where one perpetrator would distract the person at the slot machine by dropping a coin on the floor and telling them they dropped one, and when they went to pick it up, the other perpetrator would grab the coin bucket or their purse if it was a woman.

Edge heard a commotion in the next row of machines and hurried over to see what was going on. It seemed one player was beating on a guy with her cane, and Edge grabbed the cane, preventing the man from getting any more of the beating. "Police officer! Ma'am," Edge said, "What's going on here?" "He tried taking my purse," she told him. The man looked at them both and just shook his head from side to side, bleeding from a cut above his left eye, blood running down the side of his face. By that time security was there, surrounding the suspect, and they had him in handcuffs. Edge couldn't help but laugh at the dude, getting beat up by an old lady. Security led the man away to the back holding area, where he probably got more of a beating than that from the old lady. They didn't like it too much when their patrons tried to steal from other patrons to satisfy their gambling habits.

Edge let them do their job and gave the woman her cane back. "Way to go, lady," Edge told her. "I don't think he will do that again," Edge said snickering. "He better not, or I'll bop him again if he tries," she said with a wide-eyed look. Edge left her to play her slot machine and continued to walk around. Since he was here, he figured to play a little himself. He walked up to a dollar machine, slid a twenty into the slot, and started playing. He pulled the lever, and a couple of sevens and a bar came up, paying a few tokens. He did it again, and the light on the machine came on; three flaming sevens showed, and he won a jackpot. The attendant came over and proceeded to write up the jackpot slip. Edge had won five thousand credits plus his own money back.

Edge took the slip to the payout window and received his check. He exited the casino and continued to walk back the way he came on his way home. It was a profitable evening for him. It was pure enjoyment. He gave an ass-beating, watched an old lady bop a thief, and won a jackpot. Not bad, he thought. He was nightdreaming again, not noticing a suspicious person behind him. "Hold up, asshole. I want all the money you just won at the casino, now!" Edge turned and looked at him standing there, hands shaking, a knife in his right hand. "Turn around and walk the other way," Edge commanded, "It's the only warning you will get. Now do it." "No way, man. You got five large, and I want it. Now hand it over—that's the only warning you're going to get before I carve you up like Sunday ham." Edge moved his coat aside and reached for his 9 mm so fast, the robber had little time to react. He pointed the weapon right at the robber's head. "Now drop the knife or I put one right into your forehead before you can even begin to swing that blade. It's kinda stupid to bring a knife to a gunfight, now isn't it?" said Edge, smiling at him. The would-be robber, his hands still shaking, dropped the blade immediately after seeing what Edge brandished.

Edge told the would-be robber to get on the ground, hands behind his head and legs crossed at the ankles. The robber complied with the instructions. Edge grabbed one hand and slapped one cuff, then the other, at the same time shoving his head into the ground for good measure. The man screamed as pain entered his head through the front and he felt wetness on his nose, probably blood. Edge sat him up, flipped his cell phone, and pressed 911 to get a patrol car to move the prisoner. He identified himself and was told a patrol car would be dispatched right away. The man's nose had swollen immediately and blood was running freely from the area. "You know, man, you broke my nose, mutha-fucka," the suspect said. "What's yer name?" Edge asked. "My name, ahhhhh, is Eddie Johnson. They call me Fast Eddie," He replied. "Well, Eddie Johnson, I guess you weren't to fast tonight," Edge said, grinning at him.

The patrol car finally showed up, and two uniformed men got out and looked at Edge and then at the prisoner. "What happened to his nose?" one officer asked Edge. "He slipped on the ice," Edge told him. "He's lyin', man. He slammed my head in the ground, man. Police brutality, man," the suspect said as the blood slowly ran from his nose. Edge tilted his head to one side with a surprised look on his face. "You know me, guys. Come on, would I do that?" he asked with a shit-eating grin on his face. The officers looked at Edge, and the one closest to Edge said, "Yea, we know you, Lieutenant. You're damn right we know you." They all proceeded to laugh. Edge proceeded to tell them about the attempted robbery, and one officer picked up the knife with a gloved hand and placed it in an evidence bag. "You guys can have the collar," Edge told them. "Thanks, Lieutenant," they said as they picked up the suspect, placed him in the back of the car, and drove away. It was now 4:00 a.m., and Edge was satisfied with the night's excitement. He went home to his bed and held Abbie until sleep overtook him.

Chapter Twenty-Two

The Hon. Rev. Townsend was sitting in Captain Eckersley's office, when Edge, Detective Cook, and Inspector Hunnington came strolling in for their shift. Edge looked like death warmed over after his night of excitement; Detective Cook looked as pretty as ever, while the inspector was yawning. The trio entered the captain's office and sat down. "The pastor here needs a copy of the case files for the bishop. He has my OK to get it," Captain Eckersley said. "I have a copy on my desk he can take on his way out," Detective Cook stated. "Look, we haven't heard hide or hair of this Jack or John or whatever we call him in a week or so. He may never come back after what the lieutenant did on his carriage. The lietenant may even have shot one of them. Nonetheless, we have to keep this investigation open. The ball's in his court now. We have to wait for his next move," the captain hammered on. "Inspector, keep us posted on the weather activity in England," Captain Eckersley said. "Yes, sir," came the reply. "There haven't been any adverse weather conditions lately as far as I know. Today there is snow scheduled for this area. I'll check the fax machine for any faxes that may have came in," the inspector said. "Let's keep an eye and ear out for anything weird or abnormal in any patterns. This guy may be unpredictable, to say the least. Dismissed. Stay safe out there," Captain Eckersley said.

Rev. Townsend took a copy of the case files from Detective Cook and left the station. He would present it to the bishop immediately. Hopefully the bishop would make this his top priority. Too many women had died, and the police needed to stop this psycho killer at all costs. If the exorcism worked, then the twenty-first century would be rid of Jack the Ripper, hopefully for good. If the bishop approved this type of ritual, he knew he would need an assistant priest. The priest he had in mind was a God-given person with the utmost authority on this subject of exorcisms. He had studied the subject for years and traveled all over the world, assisting exorcists in getting demons to exit their hosts. His name was Rev. Jack Crenshaw. But he would wait for the bishop's decision on the matter.

John (Jack) had entered again through a quick thunderstorm in London and had brutally murdered another prostitute. He was still here and had hidden his carriage in a condemned garage on Cleveland Avenue near Sixteenth

Street. The body was sitting up in his carriage, as if to keep him company. He wasn't really finished with her just yet. He wanted to send the police, especially Detective Cook, another gift. John (Jack) took out his knife, sliced her breasts off one at time, and placed them in a box. He had to use a bigger cigar box, since they wouldn't fit in a regular cigar box. This time he carved Abbie's name on each breast—he carved Abbie on one breast and Cook on the other breast. He had an obsession with her, since he could not kill her or would not kill her. The breasts were small in size, probably a "B" cup, but he enjoyed it all the same. He opened the carriage storage compartment and removed some parcel paper and glue. Placing the box on the parcel paper, he proceeded to wrap his work for the detective. He also inserted a note in the box—a special message just for her. He would have Angus drop it off, since his wound was healing nicely.

Inspector Hunnington had grabbed the faxes and walked into the conference room where Edge and Detective Cook were playing grab-ass. Edge was still a horndog, and he was teasing Detective Cook. The inspector walked in, "I hope I'm not interrupting anything, but I received a fax from London, and there was a freak thunderstorm last night. Let's hope he didn't enter through it. If he did, he's still here because it was a quick one, so he wouldn't have been able to get back," The inspector said. Edge looked at him and his smile diminished quickly. Edge didn't look happy. Neither did Detective Cook because she could be in danger if John (Jack) decided to come after her. "If this killer is still here, he would have to hide somewhere. An abandoned building or a garage or a warehouse. He would have to hide his carriage. If he has a victim, she would be with him until he could get the fog cover to dispose of her," Edge stated. "It gives us time if we assume he has entered," the inspector said. Edge ran into the captain's office and proceeded to tell the captain about the information they had just received. The captain grabbed the phone, got the traffic captain on, and relayed this important information.

Traffic Captain Arthur Mueller issued an APB (All Points Bulletin) to all cars to be on the look out for a fog-like apparition that seemed unusual in nature. Also, he ordered to check out all abandoned warehouses, condemned garages, and buildings for anything suspicious. He had to call Judge Windham for the search warrants. He pressed the speed dial to the judge's chambers, hoping he would still be there. It was 9:00 p.m., and the judge could be working late since his caseload was heavy. "Judge Windham's office," the assistant said. "This is Captain Mueller in the traffic division, and I need to talk to Judge Windham stat," the captain said urgently. "I'm sorry but Judge Windham has left for the evening," came her reply. "It's a matter of life and death. It concerns the ripper case. I need warrants like yesterday. Please tell me where I can find him," the captain said frantically. "I'm sorry, sir, but I am not permitted to divulge that information," was her reply again. The captain slammed the receiver down in her ear and called Captain Eckersley in the detective bureau. "Captain Eckersley here." "Hey Art, this is Arthur Mueller here, and I am unable to get the warrants. The bitch in the judge's office won't tell me where he is," the traffic captain told him. "Thanks, Mueller. I'll deal with it. Good-bye." They both hung up, and Captain Eckersley motioned to Edge to come into his office. After hearing what his captain had to say, Edge knew what to do.

Edge jumped into his squad car and sped over to the courthouse just as Judge Windham's assistant was leaving for the evening. She was standing at her vehicle, when Edge approached her. "Hey lady, Lieutenant Woodredge from homicide, and I need to know where the judge is now!!" he said hurriedly. "I'm sorry, but I have strict instructions from His Honor not too say where he is this evening," she replied. "Look it lady, if you don't tell me where he is, I'll arrest you for obstruction, ya got it?" Edge told her, reaching for his handcuffs. "OK, OK, he's with the mayor at the clubhouse having a closed meeting and dinner. He is also with a couple of council members. I didn't tell you, OK?" "Your secret's safe with me, lady. Thanks," Edge said and headed for the only clubhouse he was aware of in the uppity section of town. Arriving at the valet parking area, he hopped out and told the valet to leave it because he would be right out. Edge walked up to the host at the dining area. "You can't just . . . Edge cut him off, shoved him aside with a "Yes, I can" reply, and headed to the judge's table. "Excuse me, Mr. Mayor, but I need Judge Windham now for some search warrants," Edge said out of breath. "Now you hear this, officer, I'm in the middle of something . . . Edge cut the judge off in mid-sentence with "And so am I," as he grabbed him by the shoulders, hoisted him up, and proceeded to place the handcuffs on him. "You'll regret this, and I'll have your badge for this," Judge Windham protested for all to hear. "Ya . . . Ya . . . Ya . . . Let's go," Edge said as he dragged the judge from his dinner.

He shoved the judge in the back of the squad car; the judge was still yelling at Edge and protesting the way he was being treated. Edge ignored his protests and arrived at the courthouse. Removing the judge from the car and walking him hurriedly up the stairs and into his office, he removed the cuffs. "I'm sorry, Your Honor, but this is a dire emergency, and I need those warrants now. It has to do with the ripper case, and we believe he is hiding in Niagara Falls in an abandoned or vacant building," Edge explained to him. "That's a lot of warrants to write, officer," Said the judge, now a bit calmer. "Well, can't you write just one warrant to cover all the buildings?" Edge asked him. "I'll do just that since you can't provide me with specific addresses." The judge sat at his desk, removed the warrant from his desk drawer, signed it, and then handed it to Edge. It read as follows: For all abandoned, vacant, and condemned buildings in and about Niagara Falls, whether they are garages, houses, or warehouses.

Signed *Judge Philip Windham.* "Thank you, Your Honor. Can I offer you a lift back to the country club or anywhere else?" Edge asked politely with a smirk on his face. "No, I reckon not. I think I'll take a cab back," the judge said.

Edge left in a hurry to get back to his office where the captain was waiting for him. He left the judge bewildered at the courthouse, thinking he must be crazy for dragging His Honor out in handcuffs, humiliating him in front of the whole clubhouse. Edge stammered in out of breath and into the skipper's office. "I got the warrant. It covers the whole city," he told the captain, breathing heavily. "You didn't rough him up too much, did you, Lieutenant?" the captain asked. "He's not a happy camper, if you know what I mean, skipper," Edge said, chuckling. "Exactly what does that mean, Lieutenant?" Captain Eckersley asked. "I kinda had to cuff him and drag him out of the country club," Edge said, smiling. "That's why I sent you, because you're a no-shit cop. A little humiliation never hurt anyone, even the judge. I'll cover your ass with the mayor. I know he'll understand. I have his authority to do whatever it takes to get this killer. Way to go, Edge," Captain Eckersley said. Edge left his office and returned to the conference room to get the inspector and Detective Cook. The captain was laughing so hard he was crying. He wished he could have been there to see the expression on the judge's face, and the mayor's face for that matter. It would have been golden.

The ripper trio left the squad room and returned to the streets to seek out the would-be killer. Where would they look? Edge figured, the run-down areas of the city. They would start at Niagara Street and begin their search. A total all cars all points bulletin was top priority. Police officers were combing the city and checking properties. If anyone was to protest, then they were instructed to call Captain Eckersley at the detective bureau. A copy of the search warrant would be issued upon request.

After an hour of checking vacant buildings on or near Niagara Street, the trio decided to change locations and concentrate on the center city area. Edge narrowed it down to a garage. Houses were out since he wouldn't be able to hide there unless it had an attached garage. As they were proceeding to begin their search on Ontario Avenue and Eighteenth Street, a call came over the radio. "Car forty-six to Lieutenant Woodredge. Over." "Lieutenant Woodredge here. Go ahead, forty-six," Edge replied. "Yea, Lieutenant, we have a situation off the alley on Welch Avenue—actually it's a garage. It seems we have a meth lab. Over." "That's a 10.4 on the meth lab. Call the narcotics boys," Edge responded. "10.4, Lieutenant." The radio was silent until the patrol car radioed for backup. "We have a 10.33 off the alley between Welch and Niagara Streets. Between nineteenth and Twenty-second Streets. All available cars respond," the voice came over. "Shit," Edge said, "Why now? There's always a glitch when we're busy." He turned on his lights and siren, hurrying to the section of town he had just left. He figured it would be better to back up the patrol car and then resume his search.

Arriving on scene, there was the patrol car, and the narcotics boys were also there. Edge and his two comrades got out of the car, walked over to the said garage, and entered the dwelling. What they saw was a huge meth lab with all the supplies for a mega operation. Edge looked at the patrolman and the narcotics boys. "What's the problem?" Edge asked. "It's wired with explosives," the patrolman responded. Inspector Hunnington was looking over the device. "It's a bloody sophisticated device," he added. "There's no timer, so it must be detonated if anyone messes with the lab," Edge noticed. Detective Cook was out by the car, talking to the other patrolman. They all left the garage, and Edge got on the radio and requested the bomb squad. "We'll wait for the bomb squad. Don't anyone touch anything in the garage," he commanded. "Evacuate the area within a five-block radius in all directions. Get a hold of all emergency response teams to help out. We need to get these people to safety." Edge's directions were quickly obeyed.

The bomb squad was quick on the scene, and they donned their gear and entered the garage. Sgt. Craig Donaldson was in charge, and Officer Amber Coleson was his assistant. They cautiously stood in front of the device and proceeded to separate the wires connecting the detonator to the C-4 explosive. First they snipped the wires connected to the lab, and then they snipped the hot wire to the device, causing it to be relatively harmless if anyone touched the lab. Sergeant Donaldson picked up the device and slowly turned and walked back to the tank. Upon placing the explosive device in the tank, he closed the door. Clearing the area of the police presence, Sergeant Donaldson detonated the bomb, and a loud explosion could be heard. He removed his bomb-suit helmet, and sweat was pouring from his head. "All clear," he said. Edge was relieved, and Inspector Hunnington said, "Job well done, Sergeant. Bloody well done." The scene was cleared, and the narcotics boys took over and began to gather the evidence. The two patrolmen busted the front door of the house and arrested two suspects. The ripper investigators climbed back into the car to continue their search for the elusive John (Jack).

Chapter Twenty-Three

Rev. Townsend was sitting across from the Honorable Bishop McNulty as he was reviewing the ripper case file. The bishop wore his reading glasses on the tip of his nose, and as he muttered an affirmative grunt now and then, the reverend's eyes widened and then closed as if in prayer. The bishop was studying the file closely, page by page. He would look up now and again with a puzzled expression, only to go back to his present task. The bishop set the file on his desk, looking at Rev. Townsend over his glasses. "It seems the police are in a serious pickle here. This John (Jack) suspect has the upper hand here. He can come into the twenty-first century at every storm—even small ones. Do you have an assistant priest in mind?" Bishop McNulty asked. "Yes, Your Eminence, I was considering Rev. Jack Crenshaw. So would that be a confirmation from Your Worship?" the reverend asked. "Well, he is an excellent choice and has the credentials for this type of service. I would say, if he agrees, you have my blessing. You know he is no spring chicken anymore, and his health may be in question. So tread lightly, and if either of you seem to be in danger, back out immediately. Understood, sir?" the bishop said, concerned. "Yes, Your Grace, it is understood perfectly. Thank you," said the reverend as he stood and kissed the bishop's ring.

Rev. Townsend left the Bishop's office and set out to locate Rev. Crenshaw. He would most likely be at St. Joseph Parish. Rev. Townsend would meet with him in person. He would have to make it quick because Crenshaw traveled extensively. He would only be in town a few days. Rev. Townsend had met the good reverend only on one other occasion when he was on a sabbatical in Baltimore, Maryland. His home parish wais there, and he had attended Rev. Crenshaw's service at St. Anthony's. He remembered him as being a short, portly gentleman with a double chin, which made him look fat. He remembered him being long-winded and having a gruff voice. He sounded a little like Alfred Hitchcock when he spoke—slow and long-drawn. Maybe he could bore this John (Jack) into leaving on his own. Rev. Townsend knew he was the right priest for the task at hand. Since he was more experienced than himself, Rev. Townsend probably would offer him the lead in the exorcism.

Rev. Townsend pulled up in front of St. Joseph's Church on Pine Avenue, only to learn that Rev. Crenshaw was staying at St. Teresa's a short distance away. He got back into his vehicle and was off to St. Teresa's on the east side of town. He finally arrived there, entered the parish through the rectory door, and was met by the caretaker since St.Teresa's was closed. "May I be of service to you, Reverend . . . ? As her voice trailed off, "Townsend," came the reply. "Yes, of course," she said. "I'm here to see Rev. Crenshaw, if I may, my child?" the reverend asked. "Right this way, please," she motioned him through a set of double doors. "He's in the back office," she said to him. Rev. Townsend walked to the back office, and there sat Rev. Crenshaw in a high-back swivel chair. He looked small in the chair. The reverend looked up in surprise and greeted his visitor. He indeed did have an Alfred-Hitchcock look to him. "May I assist you with something?" he asked as he rose from his high-back chair and extended his hand in friendship. "Rev. Crenshaw is my name, and yours is?" "My name is Rev. Townsend, sir, and I'm hoping you can be of assistance, sir. I need someone of your expertise with a problem we are having here in the Falls—an exorcism, sir." Rev. Townsend then told him about John (Jack) and the dilemma the police were having catching him or sending him into oblivion. Rev. Crenshaw listened with extreme curiosity and a degree of enthusiasm. The reverend finished his story and sat there gazing around the room. "What do you think about it, Rev. Crenshaw? It's strange, I know, but we are looking for a course of action for this problem," Rev. Townsend said, leaning back on his chair. "I have read the papers while I'm here and listened to the news, and it's quite a complicated case. The police have no other avenue to turn to. Maybe we can try to exorcise him. It may work, and then again, not all exorcisms do the job. He may come back at a later year. I can understand that the police don't want to alter the course of history, but he has already done that by appearing here and committing crimes—heinous crimes at that. All right, I'll stay in town until we rid Niagara Falls of Jack the Ripper." the reverend ended the long-drawn conversation. "Thank you, my good friend, and have a blessed day," Townsend said to him. "Amen to that," was his reply.

Edge was driving crazily around the city with Inspector Hunnington in the front seat and Detective Cook in the back, following leads from other patrol officers, and they all turned out to be wild goose chases. "He's got to be here somewhere," Edge said. "If he's here at all," said Detective Cook. Inspector Hunnington just sat there and looked for empty garages. He wasn't sure one way or the other if the killer was in fact here. Hopefully he wasn't. "Oh! He's here all right," Edge said. "How do you know that for sure?" Cook asked from the back. "Because he likes it—he likes carving up women. He won't let any opportunity pass him by—even small ones," Edge retorted. A call came over the radio for Lieutenant Woodredge to see the man on Cleveland Avenue about strange noises coming from his neighbor's property.

Edge and company were a block away and would take the call. Probably another wild goose chase. They arrived in front of 1619 Cleveland Avenue and went next door to talk to the complaining neighbor. The neighbor was coming up his driveway and motioned them to be quiet with a forefinger to his lips. Edge identified himself and the others as police officers and waited for his story. "I hears them strange noises comin' from that garage next door, like horses. You knows what I mean, offica'?" the neighbor said quietly. "And I ain't drunk either." "OK," Edge said, "let us take a look. Stay clear in case there is anything to your story, and there might be some shooting." Edge figured the old guy may have had one too many Budweiser's and thought he heard horses. "Inspector, you go around to the second door, and I'll take the other door. Abbie, you back us up off to my side." They slowly proceeded to the garage doors, and Edge looked at Hunnington. "It's unlocked," he said. The inspector tried to open the door but was unable to since the garage was a little shaky, to say the least. "Lift up on the handle and pull toward you and see if it moves," Edge told him quietly.

Inside the garage, Angus and John (Jack) were preparing to run the horses as fast as they could after the door opened. They had a clear driveway for an attempted escape. John was staring at his work in the seat across from him and admiring what he had accomplished. He was not afraid of any Bobbies from America. He outsmarted Scotland Yard, and he would outthink the Falls police. The door finally opened, and Angus slapped the reins on the horse's backsides; they began to bolt and run. Angus kept on slapping the reins, and the horses knocked Edge and the inspector over exiting the garage. Abbie had her weapon drawn on the carriage but couldn't fire. She was shaking, and her thoughts were of what happened to her on that night. Edge and Inspector Hunnington got up from the ground and ran to the car, with Edge stopping midway and peering back at Abbie. "Come on, Abbie, let's go. We have to catch him now!" he yelled for her. She couldn't move and just stood there. Maybe she was still under John's power. Edge ran to her and held her tight. "I'm sorry, Edge, I just couldn't shoot. I'm sorry, I'm sorry," she said as he led her to the car. "It's all right now, I'm here. Don't worry, he can't hurt you anymore. I'll take you back to the apartment where you can rest."

They all got into the car and drove back to Edge's apartment, where he helped Abbie up the stairs and put her to bed. The carriage was out of sight and hidden again. Edge would have his day when John (Jack) would not escape. This was the promise he made to himself. The inspector just nodded at Edge and returned to the car. Edge would have chased the carriage, but Abbie was in distress and he had to think of her first. He decided in her best interests that she would not come with him again until she received some counseling or reversed hypnosis. Edge returned to the car with the inspector waiting for him.

Edge climbed back into the driver's seat and looked at the inspector. "She's shot, you know that, Hunnington," he said. "We almost had him, Edge," the inspector said.

It was beginning to snow pretty heavily, and it was after 3:00 a.m., so Edge decided to take Hunnington back to the hotel for the evening. He dropped him off and bid him a good evening. Edge then drove around the city to try and locate John (Jack). The snow was big, crystallized flakes, which he referred to as Christmas snow. It was a great time of year, but not this year, since the snow would mask any tracks made by the carriage and would also hide John (Jack) from view. Again he eluded them. Edge drove over to Goat Island and parked his cruiser at the site where John (Jack) might appear to try to return to his own time. His hunch would prove correct. Edge was sitting there smoking a ciggy, when he heard the sound of hooves in the snow and a man yelling "Yeeeeaaah" at the horses. Edge ducked down in the front seat as the carriage rolled up not far from him. The carriage stopped and just sat there, probably waiting for the next lightning bolt to take them home. Edge peeked above the side window glass and noticed how eloquent the carriage looked. He had never really got a good look at it before now. It was a pretty nice carriage, very different from what the Amish drove on the roads.

Edge rolled down the window and flicked the cigarette out into the snow. He wasn't sure if he was spotted yet, as the driver was looking around. His top hat was covered in snow, as was his cape. He appeared to be a snowman in the driver's seat. Edge figured John (Jack) was in the passenger part of the carriage. He pulled the car's door handle quietly and opened the door. Stepping out, he left the door ajar so as not to alarm his suspects. Edge drew his 9 mm Smith & Wesson and trained it on the unsuspecting driver. "Freeze! (Bad pun, he thought) And step down from the carriage. Driver, put yours hands where I can see them and climb down from the carriage now!" Edge ordered, with his weapon still focused on him. Angus was startled and surprised at this outcome. He complied with the instructions and stepped down, writhing in pain as he landed on his wounded leg. "Turn around and place your hands on the carriage; and don't move or I'll shoot you dead right where you stand," Edge commanded. He went to open the carriage door, and as he was grasping the handle, a sharp pain rang in his head from John's (Jack's) cane. He fell to the ground as John continued to bring his cane down on Edge's head and body. He hit Edge's hand that was holding the nine and dislodged it, which fell under the carriage. Edge was in a daze and barely able to see John as the snow was getting into his eyes. Angus, at this point, began to kick Edge in the head and back, bringing Edge's conscious level to a breaking point. Edge was now unconscious and vulnerable. "That's enough, my friend, I don't want to kill him. Let's go. I have completed my work here," John (Jack) said as he stared at Edge's snow-covered body. Angus climbed aboard and drove away.

Edge woke to a voice asking him if he was all right. It was Niagara Parks police officer, Stan Pierce. He wasn't sure if Edge was in a drunken stupor or what had happened. Edge grabbed his head and shook off the snow. "Where is my gun? Have you seen my gun?" Edge asked wearily. "No, I haven't, sir," Officer Pierce replied. Edge got up and started kicking the snow around to look for his weapon, as did Officer Pierce. After a few minutes of shoving the snow through their feet, Officer Pierce had located the weapon. He gave it to Edge, and he began telling Officer Pierce what had happened. "Maybe you should go to the hospital and get checked out. You may have a concussion or something more serious," Officer Pierce explained. Officer Pierce radioed for assistance using the "officer down" police code. Police sirens could be heard, and the police arrived within minutes of the call. They closed off the area to everyone except the paramedics who arrived shortly thereafter. They checked Edge out, and again he refused to go to hospital. Edge walked over to Officer Pierce. "Check out the Three Sisters Islands, and take back up with you. I need to know what you find. The guy who ambushed me came from that direction. Edge's head was wringing with pain, and his eyes showed his discomfort.

Officer Pierce and four other officers proceeded to the Three Sisters Islands with flashlights gleaming through the snow and their eyes straining to see ahead of them. They had to be careful because one slip near the banks could spell doom for any one of them, since the current was too swift and ice built up on the banks, causing slippery conditions. They didn't find anything on the first two islands, but on the third they found a grisly scene—half covered in snow was the body of a young female, probably in her early twenties, slumped near a tree near the water's edge. Officer Pierce radioed for the paramedics to hurry over, and an officer was sent to guide them to the bloody scene. They arrived and set up battery-powered lights around the body and the apparently deceased female. The paramedics called the coroner. The scene was sealed and taped off. An officer was standing guard.

Officer Pierce had returned to Edge to check on his condition. "What did you find, Pierce?" Edge asked. "We found a female slumped against a tree, very dead, sir," he replied. "Was there anything missing, like body parts? Did you notice?" he again asked, still clinging to his head. "Couldn't tell, sir—too much snow covering the area," Officer Pierce replied. The CSI command unit arrived just behind the coroner. The coroner pronounced the female deceased in suspicious circumstances. There was definitely foul play. Charlie Mort saw Edge at the crime scene and inquired as to what happened to him. Edge explained that he was ambushed and he just received some bumps and bruises. "I had him again, Charlie. I had his driver standing tall against the carriage, and I let myself get ambushed," Edge was telling him. "It's not your fault, Edge—this snowstorm gave him the advantage. Don't blame yourself. Let me bag up this body, and I'll talk to you later if you feel up to it," Charlie said. "Thanks, pal," Edge came back.

Edge left the scene and let everyone do their jobs. He went to his car, sat there, lit a cigarette, and cracked open a fresh bottle of Coors Light. He took a long drink, taking the bottle prematurely from his lips and spilling some of its contents onto his overcoat. He watched as the flashlights were roaming through the trees and snow. It looked like a laser-light show. The snow was still coming down pretty heavy, and Edge decided it was time to call it a night. He didn't seem cold, except for the beer of course, and it did taste awfully good, probably one of the best tastings he had had in a while. This night didn't disappoint him; maybe Abbie did, but not the night. The second night in a row, full of excitement. He inserted the key into the ignition, and the engine came to life. He turned on the heater, and it made an awful racket like the fan was hitting something. His thoughts were of Officer Pierce finding him when he did, because this snowfall was heavy and he would have definitely been a snow drift if the officer hadn't come along. Edge was lucky tonight, or the good Rev. Townsend sent him a guardian angel. Edge put the vehicle in gear and drove home.

Chapter Twenty-Four

Abbie woke about 1:00 p.m. the next day to find Edge fully clothed in bed with her. She noticed the back of his head had a big contusion, and some dried blood was evident. She had not known what happened to him since she was out of it the previous day. She was feeling a heavy guilt complex for not firing on the carriage. This may be why Edge had been hurt, or maybe he just got into a fight to ease some stress. Either way she was concerned, but dared not wake him for fear that he would be in a mean mood. He reeked of beer, so he must have had a few too many, or a few too many had him. She slowly slid from the bed and walked to the kitchen where she began to make coffee and cook a little lunch before Edge woke up. The coffee smell filled the apartment as she poured a cup for herself. Edge was stirring, and soon he would be waking for the day.

John (Jack) had claimed his fifth victim at Three Sisters Islands, and this one was his worst yet. Charlie had cleaned the body and was inspecting it for any unusual markings, missing organs, and what not. She was a mess and purely unidentifiable. She had no face at all. Her breasts had been removed and her pubic area totally disfigured, as if a maniac had gone crazy on this young woman in a way of total hatred. Charlie was sick looking at this lump of flesh. There wasn't a part on her that wasn't sliced up. Her large intestine was outside of the body, and some of her toes were missing. It was like he was a shark in a feeding frenzy. All her fingers were cut off as if he didn't want her identified. This was a forensic nightmare. He placed the x-ray machine in position and began to do a total body scan, especially the head, possibly to get an ID from dental records. He could take thumbprints, but maybe she was never fingerprinted. They wouldn't be too much use to him, but he would do it anyway. The coroner couldn't even believe what he was seeing. He had never seen anything like this before. This was a total disregard for a human existence. Whoever did this horrendous act was purely evil. He had no mind or soul. He saw nothing but death. His hatred for women knew no bounds. When the snow melted, they would have to find her fingers and toes, unless they were taken as trophies. Charlie had made the sign of the cross above the woman and placed her in the cold storage area until her identity could be found. Maybe he would check missing persons.

Edge had awakened to Abbie moving around the apartment and the smell of the coffee brewing. "Hey sweetie, a cup of that smell would go awful good right about now," Edge hinted to her. She poured him a cup of hot black coffee, which was the way he liked it, and handed it to him. "Are you going to tell me what happened last night, or do I have to play twenty questions?" she asked. "Why don't you lighten up a little—I have a headache, and my body aches," he retorted. "What did you do—go out and get drunk last night?" Abbie looked at him with a hand on her hip. "I wish I did, but it didn't happen that way. John (Jack) claimed another victim last night, and he ambushed me. If it hadn't been for the Parks police officer coming when he did, I'd be a snow bank by now." Edge proceeded to tell her what happened, how he had the driver up against the carriage, and how he was ambushed from behind. She sat there motionless, taking an occasional sip of her coffee and listening to the story. She then became sympathetic and began kissing him all over his face. "Hey, watch that bump on my head—it's still tender," Edge winced a little. "I'm sorry, baby. I'm sorry for not firing on the carriage. Maybe if I would have done my job instead of freezing up, this might not have happened," she said guiltily. "Don't blame yourself for any of this. I was assuming that John (Jack) was in the carriage, and I would have had them both. But he wasn't. That's my fault for making an ass out of myself. It had nothing to do with you. I gotta get into the shower and get some fresh clothes on." Edge took his last gulp of coffee and headed for the shower.

Inspector Hunnington had left the hotel and walked over to Edge's apartment, which was a short distance away. He knocked, and Abbie opened the door, inviting him in. "Cup of coffee, Inspector? Or tea, perhaps?" she asked him. "No, nothing for me, thanks," he replied. Edge was still in the shower, and Abbie asked him to have a seat while they both were getting ready for their day's shift. She started by telling him what had happened to Edge in the early morning hours. The inspector's face was expressionless and not surprised at what he was hearing. He knew this killer would do whatever it took to evade capture. He felt as though he was back in John's (Jack's) time and was the lead investigator on the case. He had to start thinking like John (Jack). They had to find a weakness in him and turn that weakness on their side.

Edge came out of the bathroom stark-naked as he was toweling off, hoping to get Abbie in the mood. To his surprise was the inspector sitting at his table. Edge just stood there stunned. "Ya kinda got me by surprise, Inspector," Edge said, wrapping the towel around his waist. "You know, Lieutenant, I kinda figured you'd be bloody bigger, is all," the inspector said, chuckling. "You're a hilarious bloke, aren't you? Ten thousand English comedians out of work, and you're trying to be one," Edge said sarcastically. "I didn't expect you, is all," Edge looked at him. "I didn't expect you to come out of the bathroom naked either," the inspector told him. "Well, it's my apartment. I guess I can come out of the bathroom any which way I want," he retorted back. Edge grabbed his clothes, headed back into his bathroom, and five minutes later was dressed. The trio walked to Edge's car and was off to the station to talk to the captain.

Angus had set the box with the breasts inside by the door of the station, out of camera view. It was addressed to Miss Abigail Cook in old French script. A patrolman coming in for his shift noticed it and immediately called the desk lieutenant on the phone outside the building. The lieutenant instructed him not to touch it until the bomb squad x-rayed it for explosive devices. Sergeant Donaldson arrived, carefully picked up the package, placed it in the portable x-ray machine, and discovered no devices. It was harmless. The sergeant picked the package up and carried it to Detective Cook's desk for when she arrived. She usually worked the evening shift with Edge, and he figured it might be pertaining to the ripper case. He was very, very right.

The ripper trio ambled in about 4:00 p.m., and immediately Detective Cook spied the package on her desk. A sudden apprehensive feeling overcame her; she looked at the other two and slowly walked over. The captain hadn't arrived yet, so she knew that he didn't put it there. "Did anyone see who put this package on my desk?" she asked. "Yea, it was Sergeant Donaldson," Detective Reyes said. "I'll open it if you want me to," Edge said to her. She called Donaldson, and he told her there was nothing in the package that was explosive. He also told her that a patrolman spotted the package by the back door. "I checked the video and nothing was on it," he explained to her. She hung up the receiver and asked Edge, "Why don't you do the honors." He put on some latex gloves and began to open the package. It was glued instead of taped. He lifted the cigar box out of the wrappings and opened the lid carefully. To his amazement, inside there were two breasts. "Nice pair," he said. Detective Cook noticed her name was carved on the breasts. She started shaking and crying uncontrollably, and Edge was there to comfort her. He was very agitated at the events that were happening to his woman. Inspector Hunnington put gloves on, picked up the letter, and began to read it. It was in old French script.

To my darling Abigail,

This is a small token of my appreciation of your beauty. I cannot kill you, but you amaze me in a way I cannot explain. I hope you will mount these on your fireplace mantel if you have one. You cannot catch me, you cannot catch me.

Sincerely, you're close
to my heart, John

Edge picked up the package and the wrappings and brought them to the lab after showing the contents to the skipper. The captain was not amused at what Edge did, because he had just finished breakfast. He put them under his nose even before he could inquire as to what was in the package. He told Edge to get out of his sight and get Abbie to the Union Psyche for evaluation. She was placed on administrative leave until further notice as per Captain Eckersley. Edge would take her the next day in the midmorning. Until then, she would shuffle papers and answer phones. Edge had told Charlie that he needed an ID on the latest victim. Charlie would check the dental records database and see what came up.

Edge looked at Inspector Hunnington and said "It looks like it's just you and I to hunt for this elusive killer." "I think we should stick together no matter what time of day it is or where we are," Inspector Hunnington announced. "I guess I can accept that conclusion, since I did get quite a beat-down by this dude," Edge elaborated. "This man is desperate, and desperate men are irrational in their thinking. This latest victim was his worst, and he's getting braver as he keeps on killing. It's like a thrill ride for him. The more he kills, the more destructible he becomes, and the worse his victims will appear to us. He will slip up and make a mistake, and we'll be right on top of him," Inspector Hunnington stated.

John (Jack) had taken the Goat Island Bridge to Buffalo Avenue and had broken into the old Promex building near the site of one of his victims. It was where he had dumped Tiara's body at the stone chimney. It was an empty building that once housed a medical production company. It was huge, so he had no problem with fitting in his carriage and horses there. It was a waiting game for the weather to change in England. The problem he had was that he had no way of knowing what the weather would be in England. The bobbies had the upper hand there. Angus was getting a bit worried that the bobbies would soon be coming to this hiding spot, and would either capture them or kill them. The one that had him up against the carriage was very smart, or just lucky. It was the same bloody goomer that shot him in the leg. They had to move. "Sir, we have to leave this dwelling—I have a bad feeling about us being here," Angus had expressed his concern to his employer. "I firmly believe you have a point, Angus. We have worn out our welcome here."

Edge and the inspector had arrived at the closed Promex building. Before entering, Edge had radioed the station and requested the SWAT team. He didn't feel like being ambushed again, and besides that, the captain had given him a stern warning about being a lone wolf on this case. The SWAT team arrived and set up a perimeter around the dwelling. Edge and his partner were waiting with Sergeant Johnson by the rear warehouse door. Johnson was to enter first as the officer with the door buster was to knock in the door. Once the door was busted in, Sergeant Johnson entered, and the rest of the team secured the building. "All secure, Lieutenant. You can enter now," Johnson said as his men had their weapons pointed in all directions of the building. Every door was covered and every room was secure. Edge and the inspector entered the building, only to find John (Jack) had left. "He was here, Edge," Inspector Hunnington noted, "The horses left some road apples on the floor." "Road apples?" Edge inquired. "What the fuck are road apples?" he asked. "You know, bloody horse crap. There's a whole pile over here." the inspector showed Edge the horse excrement. "Why didn't you just say horse shit? I would have understood that better," Edge said smiling. "OK, Sergeant, let's get this place locked up and taped off. It just became a crime scene. Come on, Inspector, let's continue our search."

John (Jack) and Angus had moved their location just in time as Edge and the inspector were hot on their trails. Angus had traveled the horses down Buffalo Avenue to a warehouse not far from their previous hideout. It was across from a closed factory and set back away from the road. The building next to it was the skeletal remains of an old storage company. The windows were broken out, and anyone who ventured there were either homeless people or drug addicts. Some years ago, they found a body there of a heroin addict who had overdosed, with the needle still in his arm. So the city gutted the building, just leaving the skeleton. John (Jack) and Angus felt more secure there. The snow had let up, and their tracks were well covered. John (Jack) felt more at ease now. They had to get back to their own time since it was getting close to another date—according to history, Jack's next killing. "Angus, tonight we leave for I have to get back to work in England. I sense a snowstorm this evening, which will let us escape. I have concluded that when there is a storm here, there must be a storm in our homeland, since they are mostly on the same longitudinal lines," John (Jack) said as he patted the horses' manes. "Very well, sir. That sounds like a bloody good idea, sir," Angus answered in kind with a worried grin on his face.

Edge was thinking about Abbie sitting at her desk, bored as hell shuffling papers and pushing a pencil. It wasn't her type of work, but she couldn't be trusted on the street because partners had to depend on one another and watch each other's back. The inspector knew Edge was nightdreaming about Abbie. "She'll be fine, Edge. She's back at the headquarters at her desk, safe and sound," he said to him. "I know, Inspector. It's just that I've been her partner since she joined the detective bureau. I could count on her. I relied on her, and now since this case has been going on, I don't know if I can rely on her to have my back ever again. She seems to be under the spell of this dude. Maybe if I can kill him, it would break the spell," Edge looked at him worriedly. "Maybe so, Edge," the inspector said softly.

Chapter Twenty-Five

Charlie Mort had identified the ripper's latest victim as Tricia Watson. She was a local girl born and raised in Niagara Falls to a well-to-do family. She was of Caucasian race and had been arrested for possession of drugs a couple of years back. She had no arrests for prostitution, but that didn't mean she wasn't hooking to support her habit. Charlie left the report on Edge's desk and went back to his lab. Abbie walked over to Edge's desk, picked up the folder, and began leafing through the pages, scanning each page briefly before she came to the pictures of the dead girl. She sat down in Edge's chair with tears in her eyes as she looked at the crime scene pictures. Tears ran down her cheeks and dripped onto the photo of the mutilated body. She had observed other bodies of homicide victims, but none as terrible as what she was looking at now. Abbie closed the folder and held it tight, as if trying to picture John (Jack) slicing this girl to shreds, and also remembering her ordeal, feeling lucky she wasn't a victim. Now he is stalking her and haunting her, not only in pictures and packages, but also in her dreams.

Captain Eckersley noticed her state of emotion, and walked out to her and handed her a tissue for her tears. "Why the tears? Abigail," the captain asked. "They just identified the latest victim, and it was awful. How could any human being do this to another human being? It's unconscionable," Abbie said, wiping her eyes. "Some people have no soul or conscious mind. They have impulses that drive them crazy. It's like a shark in a feeding frenzy. They just react to their sense of mind and are driven by this to kill, or in this case, mutilate their prey. Hookers are prey to this killer, and the more he kills, the better he likes it. It's a domination thing. Something must have triggered this maniacal mechanism in him to perform these hideous crimes. Why don't you go home and take some time off? We can handle things here. Take a leave of absence. Edge will keep you informed of any breaks in the case," he said, sounding sympathetic. Detective Reyes approached at the motioning of the captain's hand. "Take Detective Cook home, and I'll explain everything to the lieutenant when he gets in," he ordered. Detective Reyes gently put his hand to the small of her back and guided her to the door. She grabbed her coat on the way out and turned and smiled at the captain as if to say thank you, without uttering the words. On the way to the car, Reyes's cell phone sounded, and it was the captain telling him to stay with her until further notice from him.

Edge and the inspector entered the squad room to pick up Detective Cook as Edge was going to take her for a liquid lunch. Maybe if she got a couple of drinks under her belt, she would feel more at ease. But to no avail; Abbie wasn't anywhere around. Maybe she was in the ladies' room? Or downstairs, running errands for the captain? Edge didn't know and became very alarmed, as did the inspector. They both hurriedly open the captain's door and stood there waiting for the captain to yell at them for not knocking first. Instead he motioned them to have a seat with a hand gesture. He opened his desk drawer and lifted three glasses out of it and a bottle of imported scotch whiskey. "You two care for a spot of nerve medicine?" he asked as he began to pour himself a shot from the bottle. Edge never had known the captain to drink on duty before, so he became apprehensive. "So, what's up, skipper?" he asked. "You look worried?" the inspector intervened. "Detective Cook saw the crime photos of the latest victim on your desk, Edge, and was visibly upset, so I sent her home with Detective Reyes. He will be guarding her until further notice. I don't want her to be alone until this case is over. Just as a precautionary measure. The mayor's been up my ass, and the chief has been singing in my ear a sad song about this ripper killer. He's sounds like a broken record." The captain took another shot of scotch, gulped it down, and then looked at the glass, twirling it around in his fingers. He set the glass down and lifted the bottle toward the both of them as if to say this is your last chance. Edge covered the glass with his hand, but the inspector picked up his glass and the captain poured him a shot. "I never turn down a good scotch whiskey," the inspector motioned to him as if toasting an occasion. He gulped the whiskey down and winced a little, feeling a slight burning as the whiskey went down his throat. "Whoa, that's bloody good stuff, Captain," he said and handed the captain the glass. The captain placed the whiskey and glasses in the top drawer of his desk.

Edge looked at the captain and noticed a tired-eyed skipper with a worried look on his face. This case was getting to him also. It was getting to everybody, especially the skipper since he had to take the heat from the upper echelon. He always told his detectives that shit rolls downhill from the upper echelon to the patrolman. It was a military term that he learned when he was in the marines. Edge couldn't believe that the captain was a marine. This Twinkie-eating man let himself go since his younger days in the marines. He joined up after high school, began his training at Camp LeJune, North Carolina, and then went on to be a marine security guard. In the navy they were called Shore Patrol; Edge wasn't sure what the marines called their security. The Secret Service wanted him in their agency, but he turned them down. He said it was too much traveling to guard the president. He came back home to Niagara Falls, entered the academy for police officer training, and worked his way up the ladder to Captain. He sat there, appearing to be a broken man, with maybe his job on the line. Edge could relate to that, since his job was almost gone when he shot Ace eight months ago. The captain stood up for him, much to his disliking of Edge's brand of police work. Nonetheless, police officers always had each other's back. Except if a cop was dirty, and then no one wanted anything to do with him. He felt the captain's pain and would do anything to catch this evil John (Jack). Inspector Hunnington could sense the urgency also.

It was getting late, and another snowstorm was in the forecast, so the captain decided it was better to leave and get a good night's sleep. All three rose from their chairs, and the captain grabbed his coat and hat and proceeded to put them on. "You two go home and get some sleep because we may be in for a busy day tomorrow. I will need fresh and alert people out there. Edge, if you decide to go about the city tonight on your adventurous travels, don't forget to call for backup and let me know about any advances in the case. I don't care what time of the night it is, let me know. I need to be in on whatever goes on. Got it?" he ordered. "Gotcha, skipper," Edge replied. "Have a good evening, sir," the inspector said. The captain left the room, and Edge and Inspector Hunnington were left standing alone in the squad room. Edge walked to his desk, picked up the folder that Charlie had left for him, and began reading the contents. Inspector Hunnington was waiting with much interest.

Edge started out by stating that her name was Tricia Watson, age 23, born in Niagara Falls, five feet even in height, and weighed 110 lbs. He used dental records to identify the victim. Edge's eyes diverted to the inspector, and he handed the folder to his now partner. As the inspector was reading, Edge began to speak in an off tone—a depressed voice, so to speak. "I have to go see her parents tomorrow afternoon and tell them. Care to come along, Inspector?" Edge asked him. "It's not one of my favorite tasks, but I will accompany you for moral support," he responded. "Let's get the hell out of here and get a beer," Edge said with a soft sigh. "A bloody good idea, if I do say so myself, Lieutenant," the inspector agreed.

They left the station, and Edge and the inspector were proceeding to leave, when a call came over the radio about a suspicious person hanging out at Oakwood Cemetery. The cemetery was located in the mid-city area on Portage Road, and Edge arrived there in seven minutes. He drove through the entrance and cruised around the curve to the huge mausoleum in the rear of the cemetery. Hunnington noticed a movement by the side of the mausoleum near the alley. Edge parked in front of the building, and they both got out, with Edge going around one side and the inspector the other. On the inspector's side was a young man sitting by the mausoleum wall with a camera and a small portable voice recorder. Edge followed a moment later. They shined their flashlights on the startled fellow, who dropped his equipment and raised his hands when Edge announced his police presence. "What did I do?" he asked, his voice shaky. "What are you doing here this time of night?" Edged asked in a stern tone. "I'm just ghost-hunting," the man said. Edge looked at the inspector, and the inspector looked at the scared man, figuring he was going to jail. "Ghost-hunting, huh!" Edge motioned, "Well, you just seen two specters right here. Now take off and don't let me catch you in here again or you're going to the ghost-hunting jail." Edge watched the man jump up, hop over the guardrail, and run down the alley, slipping and falling on the ice several times.

Edge and Inspector Hunnington walked to the car which was still running, got in, and took off, having taken care of the ghost-hunter. Edge drove over to Third Street, but the British Pub had already closed, so he took off to the Quality Inn and dropped the inspector off out in front. "I bid you a good evening, Lieutenant. It was interesting. I'm surprised you didn't arrest him for criminal trespass," the inspector said with a chuckle. "What would the other charge be? Ghost-hunting?" Edge said with a grin. "Catcha later, muffin boy," said Edge, now laughing. The inspector just shook his head from side to side as he entered the hotel. He retired to bedlam.

Edge drove away, spinning his tires in the ice and snow, and fishtailed around the corner to Third Street. He got out of the car, locked the doors, and walked up the long flight of stairs to his apartment. He unlocked his door and noticed that Detective Reyes was sitting in front of the TV, watching "The Cops" show. "Hey, Reyes," Edge said softly. "What's going on, Edge?" Reyes returned. "How's she doing? Is she sleeping?" he asked. She's been restless a bit, but everything has been quiet," Reyes told him. "I think it's time for you to go and get some sleep. I'll be here the rest of the night. I'll see you later, and thanks for being here. Come back by about 3:00 p.m." Edge said, looking at Abbie sleeping in his room. Detective Reyes picked up his coat, put it on, turned to Edge, and said, "Take care, Lieutenant, and have a good evening. See you a little later." Reyes then opened the door and left.

Edge stood there watching Abbie and wondering what kind of spell this John (Jack) had over her. He took off his coat and clothes and lay beside Abbie without disturbing her. He lay there with his eyes open, staring at the ceiling, until sleep took over. Sounds of horse's hooves could be heard out on Third Street, and wagon wheels were loudly evident until they seemed to stop in front of Edge's apartment. The horses shook their heads as the snow began to accumulate on their manes. The carriage just sat there in front of the building, quietly. A tall figure dressed in black with a tall hat stood motionless on Edge's balcony, peering into the room. He raised one hand almost above his head as if to guide his Abbie to join him again. Abbie rose from the bed, dressed only in her nightgown, and proceeded over to John (Jack). As she was about to reach this figure, Edge sat straight up in bed and looked on Abbie's side. She lay there sleeping peaceably. Edge looked over at the balcony, and there was no figure standing there and no carriage out front. "Wow, that was some nightmare. The bastard's inside my head now," he whispered to himself. He sat on the edge of the bed and looked at the clock. It was 4:00 a.m. He had only been asleep for an hour or so. The nightmare seemed so real. Edge got up and lit a cigarette, walked to the balcony, and watched Third Street a while before tossing the ciggy out.

He turned and began walking back to the bed and noticed black rose on Abbie's side next to her head. He grabbed his weapon and started a search of his apartment. There was no John (Jack) or anyone else for that matter. Where did the rose come from? The bastard must have been here? Who could have left the rose but him? Edge grabbed his jeans and shoes, ran for the door, down the stairs, and to the car. He put the key in the ignition and geared the vehicle down the snow-covered street in search of any sign or tracks made by the carriage and horses. He traveled around Goat Island when the weather changed suddenly from a snowstorm to a wet rain with thunder and lightning. Edge looked toward the sky when a huge lightning strike appeared to hit the island. He knew then that John (Jack) returned to England.

Chapter Twenty-Six

Edge drove back to his apartment, freezing his ass off since his hurry at getting out of the building was imminent and was trying to get John (Jack). He was shirtless as he just grabbed his jeans and sneakers. He got out of his car, and when he was about to walk to his door, a patrol car came up the street, not recognizing Edge at first, rolled down the window, and shouted "Hey feller, you feeling right in the head being out here with no shirt or coat on?" Edge turned and looked in the direction of the shouting and noticed it was Officer Thompson. "No Thompson I'm not all right," Edge replied. "Hey lieutenant, I didn't recognize you at first," Officer Thompson said. Edge was standing there with his weapon in his waistband and was shaking uncontrollably. "So, what gives? Lieutenant Woodredge," he asked. "I was chasing a murder suspect," Edge told him. "I suggest you get inside before you catch your death out here," the officer told him. "Brilliant, thanks for your thoughts, see you later, Thompson" Edge ran inside and up the stairs, stripped his skivvy shorts, climbed under the blankets, and drifted off to sleep.

John (Jack) was safely back in England. He entered the White Chapel area of London, where his next victim would be discovered that evening. Angus was busy digging the horse's hooves of ice and snow with a special awl that curved around the shoe and would release the ice in one big chunk. The horses seemed to welcome what he was doing. John (Jack) exited the carriage and walked to the front and stood in front of Angus, who continued his duties, not even looking up to inquire what his employer wanted. He was cold and didn't really care at this point. All he was thinking about was getting back to the carriage house and taking care of the carriage and the horses. He figured that after he was finished, he would invade his bosses brandy and drink himself into a drunken stupor. "Angus, I will be at the inn for a while and then I will be at the mansion for a change of clothes. Have them ready for me, will you, my good man?" John (Jack) asked. "Yes my lord, I will lay them out in the master bedroom for when you return" Angus said with a sense of anger in his voice. John (Jack) left Angus to his business and proceeded walking through the White Chapel area, where he had an apartment to spend the evening. His apartment was located on Hanbury Street and was an easy access when he finished his murderous tasks. He arrived at his apartment and threw off his hat and cape on the bed along with his cane. He sat at the table and began to write his memoirs in letters to Scotland Yard, tempting them to catch him.

Angus returned to the mansion, stabled the horses, and made sure they had plenty of grain. The carriage was parked in the drive just outside the stables. He entered the mansion and climbed the long winding staircase to the second-floor rooms. He opened the master bedroom, went to the closet, and removed the next day's garments for his master. He laid them neatly on the bed. He then went to the master's den, removed a bottle of his best brandy, put it in his coat, and left for his own quarters, which was located behind the stables and carriage house. It was a small one-room cottage with a table, a bed, and a nice size fireplace on the back wall. He found it comfortable. He lit the fire in the fireplace with some newsprint and logs and soon the fire was roaring and his place was warm. He sat at the table and began to drink the brandy. He chose brandy over the sherry because he thought the sherry was too sweet and it was a sissy drink. He sipped the brandy from the bottle and the it went down smooth, not burning his throat like some of the rye he had tasted. He kept sipping from the bottle, and the sips got longer and longer and before he knew it, his head hit the table. He was out cold drunk.

In his apartment, John (Jack) changed into his what he called his beggar's clothes and went to the inn for a couple of brandies. On his way, he came across a young lady, standing in the shadows. He looked in her direction, which gave her the notion he was interested. She approached where he was standing and gave him her best sensuous look and her sexiest strut. "How's the goods? Govna," she asked with a broad smile as she felt the lower portion of his trousers. He stepped back a bit surprised by her hand in his crotch area. "I'm well . . . ," he said, a shy sort removing her hand and touching his face lightly. "I can remedy that for you if you so desire," she motioned in the direction of the shadow where she was first noticed. As she turned and began to walk away holding his hand, John (Jack) reached into his right pocket and grabbed a knife. He walked with her until she was in the shadows and then grabbed her around the throat, slitting it from ear to ear, cupping her mouth with his left hand until all he heard was a gurgling sound, and then felt the warm blood running down his arm and hand until it landed on her chest. The arterial spray went in every direction until her body slumped to the ground motionless. He slit open her abdomen and removed her large intestine, which he set atop her chest area. He removed her liver and placed it in his overcoat pocket for future teasing of Scotland Yard.

John (Jack) left the scene, closing his coat and wiping his hands off with his handkerchief along with his face as not to show any blood on himself, and entered the pub and ordered his brandy. Sitting at the pub, he heard screaming from another lady of the evening. It was a long drawn out scream of irrational behavior and many more followed. His face was expressionless and the curdled screams affected everyone in the pub but him. Everyone rushed to see what the commotion was. He already knew. It didn't take long for anyone to find her. Scotland Yard was ready on the scene and their investigation began. Inspector Abberline and several other constables were standing around the body, asking if anyone knew who she was. A young prostitute came forward and stated, "Her name is Annie Chapman." Inspector Abberline turned and began to question the woman. She was the one who discovered the body. She had much less calm down except for an occasional sob.

John (Jack) was standing in the rear of the crowd, not even being noticed to what he had done. A smile pursed his lips as he walked away to his Hanbury Street apartment. In his apartment, he disrobed and threw the beggars clothes into the fire. He cleaned off his knife and slipped it back into its sheath. He picked up his black pants and put them on along with his dirty white shirt and black vest. He slipped his overcoat on over the vest and clasped his cape on, picking up his cane and placing his top hat squarely on his head; he exited the Hanbury Street place and began his lonely walk to the mansion, passing by the crime scene again and whistling the Minute Waltz tune that he adored. He had a letter in his pocket to Scotland Yard, which he dropped into the letter receptacle. The whistling could be heard down Hanbury Street until he was out of sight.

Edge had waked up to the knock at his door, which was probably Detective Reyes. The same knock also woke Abbie, and she sat up startled looking around the room. Edge got up from the bed in his skivvy shorts and opened the door, and indeed, it was Detective Reyes. "Com' on in Reyes," as Edge held the door for him. "You look like you're ready for the day, Lieutenant?" Reyes said laughing. Edge said, "shut up, Reyes, I've had a trying night chasing after this ripper dude," looking at him tiredly. "Abbie will be right out, she's getting dressed. Do me a big favor and keep her here in the apartment. Do not let her go anywhere, not even to the store. You order your food in and if you need anything, you can call me and I'll bring whatever you need over. She has to be protected at all costs. Saavy," Edge looked at him sternly. "Yes Sir, I saavy every word lieutenant," Reyes replied.

Abbie exited the bathroom and sat on the couch in the living room, a small distance from where Reyes was. "Hey Reyes, I see you got babysitting duty again?" she said to him. Reyes just smiled and nodded. Edge was in the bathroom and he took a navy shower, this time remembering to come out with clothes on. Toweling his hair and tossing the towel aside, his hair resembled a bad hair day. He brushed his fingers through his hair in a combing motion and put on a winter Buffalo Bills stocking cap. He threw a little stink on and grabbed his coat, and giving Abbie a kiss on the cheek and a quick stern look at Reyes, he went out the door to pickup Inspector Hunnington.

The inspector was waiting in front of the hotel as he watched Edge drive up, opening the door, he sat down in the passenger seat. "I bid you welcome lieutenant," the inspector said. "I had a busy evening last night. The ripper was in my apartment and left Abbie a black rose. I chased him to Goat Island where he supposedly went back to his own time. He was in my apartment Inspector. What the hell happened to the weather reports from Scotland Yard?" Edge was fuming. The inspector was just as surprised as Edge and he would get to the bottom of the problem. He looked at Edge worriedly, "I will take care of it as best I can lieutenant as soon as I get to the station." Edge drove away and headed to the Gazette to talk with his reporter friend Andy Blair. Edge parked in front of the Gazette and walked through the door to the receptionist's desk, up the stairs to Andy's office. Andy was standing there reviewing the next day's stories he had to run. He looked up and saw Edge coming toward him. He set his stories down as he greeted Edge; "How are you doing lieutenant?" Andy asked. "I need a small favor, Andy" was his reply. "I need you to run a fake story about the ripper. If he reads the paper here, he'll be really pissed off at what I'm about to ask you to print. I need you to print a story that the ripper case is closed," he continued. "Whoa! That's a tall order Edge, but I think I can manage it," Andy said to him. "Thanks Andy, see you later," Edge left and returned to the car.

The inspector was curious as to what Edge was thinking or about what he was going to do. With that thought in mind, they drove to the station and Inspector Hunnington quickly went to the fax machine and retrieved the faxes from London. Searching the faxes, he came across one weather report that stated severe weather this evening in both parts of the world. He relayed this information to Edge and that set up the current events in motion. The plan was on its way. Edge had to call the good Reverend and have him set up his exorcism ritual. Edge was in Captain Eckersley's office going over the said plan to catch this despicable killer. He knew that John (Jack) couldn't resist not coming back tonight, but you never know because there were always surprises.

Rev. Townsend had just got off the phone with Edge and the plan was a go. He had to contact Rev. Crenshaw and get prepared for this evening's ritual. They were optimistic about tonight because there wasn't a demonic possession so to speak. This was keeping a demon killer out of their time. A killer that claimed five victims here, and God only knows how many in his own time. He was an elusive spectre as one could only fathom in a paperback novel, so they would try to exorcise this evil, hopefully to keep him in own time.

Rev. Townsend jumped into his car and drove over to St. Teresa's and parked behind the church. He entered through the back door, which was closest to the Rev. Crenshaw's Quarters and walked up the stairs. The door to his office was open and he was seated at his desk. Startled by his appearance, Rev. Crenshaw looked at him with a high brow look and motioned him to enter. He was preparing this week's sermon titled "Don't give up the Ship." "Hello Rev. Townsend, How are you doing this afternoon?" he asked. "I just received a phone call from Lieutenant Woodredge and he informed me of a major storm tonight and he feels that this killer will be coming through this evening. He would like us to be prepared to conduct the ritual. What do you think about this?" "What time would he like us to be there and where to meet him? We need some work done first before we can get on with this. First of all, I need the area cleared of all snow down to the pavement and a large circle big enough to encase the carriage. We have to pour salt around the area to keep the carriage there. He may not be in the carriage, so we have to be prepared for that. Some demons will disguise themselves as not to be recognized. Are you ready for this?" Rev. Crenshaw asked. "I am as ready as I will ever be" came his reply.

I have to prepare myself with a service to the lord, and you can contact Lieutenant Woodredge and prepare the area where you think he may come through. Rev. Townsend then left the office and returned to police headquarters to speak with Edge. Rev. Crenshaw entered St. Teresa's sanctuary and began the writ of exorcism, starting with his own cleansing and purification and ending with a communion service. After the purification process was complete, he was to bless the holy water and the crosses he would need.

Rev. Townsend sat at Edge's desk waiting for Edge to exit the captain's office. He wasn't sure if this type of ritual would work, since there was no demonic possession, just an evil human being if you could call him one. This evil entity had no rhyme or reason to kill, just a much liking to do so. Just the same he had to be eradicated from the twenty-first century never to return. Edge looked out from the skipper's office and noticed the reverend sitting at his desk. The captain told Edge he wasn't too keen on bringing in civilians to assist in police work for fear of them getting injured or even killed. Edge had explained to him that the pastors were very willing to assist in any way they could. The captain looked out and motioned Rev. Townsend to come in. "You know this could be dangerous to you and the other pastor. Are we clear on that, Sir?" Captain Eckersley asked. "Yes sir, we are clear on the dangers in this investigation," Rev. Townsend replied. "Very well, let's get on with this then" the captain said as he looked at them both. Rev. Townsend left to join Rev. Crenshaw, and Edge left to his desk to prepare the S.W.A.T. team, but first, he was going to call Abbie at his apartment.

Chapter Twenty-Seven

The next days headline at the Gazette read as follows:

> RIPPER CASE CLOSED!
> Lt. Neil Woodredge of the Niagara
> Falls Police Department has
> announced today that the case of
> the Falls Ripper has been closed
> and placed in the cold case file.
> The investigation has ended.

The story went on and explained his decision on the most prominent story in the city's history. He knew calls would be coming in as this story hit the press. He just wanted one person to see it and hoped he would. Maybe his ego wouldn't let him go back until he would commit more murders. Maybe he would stick around long enough to be caught or sent back for good. These thoughts were a shot in the dark, but worth the gamble. He needed time and John (Jack) would give it to him. The ladies of the evening were still in protective custody. They bitched and moaned about their rights being violated, but at least they were alive to trick another day.

Edge had called Abbie to see how she was holding up not being a part of the investigation. Being in protective custody was not to her liking but necessary for her mental survival. The phone rang and rang and rang with no answer to his call. He recalled that he gave strict instructions to Reyes not to leave her or take her anywhere. He thought it strange that Reyes would disobey his orders, so he hopped into the car and drove over to his apartment. Arriving, he ran up the stairs and noticed his apartment door was partially open. He withdrew his weapon and moved the door to open all the way, checking behind it, and his breathing was heavier now after running up the stairs and his adrenalin was rushing through his system as his weapon was ready for what he was about to find. He checked his bathroom and bedroom, both were empty. His living room was also empty with the television still on to tru t.v. His curtains on the balcony were closed, which he thought was unusual. He swept the curtains with one hand, while his weapon was trained on any surprises he may incur.

He noticed Detective Reyes was sitting in a chair with his throat garroted and his white shirt was crimson stained. He felt for a pulse, but there was none. Detective Reyes was dead. Could John (Jack) have done this? He didn't think so since it was not his forte.

Edge called the station and asked for Captain Eckersley and an ambulance to his apartment. He also ordered the crime scene investigators. He knew Charlie Mort would be here on the case since him and Reyes were close. Where was Abbie? He sat waiting for the people he had just called with his 9 mm resting on his knee. He could hear the sirens in the distance getting closer and closer until they pulled out in front. First to arrive was Captain Eckersley and he walked over to examine the body of Detective Reyes. The detective was sitting upright in the chair with his head tilted back on the chair with his throat wide open. The garrote was still present dangling from both sides. The captain walked around the body with a tear in his eye, as the blood was still dripping down on the floor. "What or who do you think did this?" he asked Edge. "I dunno skipper. I don't think it was the ripper though. It may have been his driver. Abbie is gone. I think the ripper has Abbie now, so that changes things a whole lot."

Charlie mort arrived with his team and he immediately began to walk to the dead detective but was stopped by Captain Eckersley with one hand. The hand was brushed aside as he looked at the captain. "I have a job to do, sir. Please do not stop me." The captain let him through and he was stunned to see what had happened to his friend and fellow investigator. It was rather gruesome to see his comrade sitting there with no life left in him. It hurt him very much. He tried to hold back his tears but to no avail, they came anyway. After he composed himself, he began his investigation and evidence collection. The coroner arrived next and Charlie filled him in on what was going on. Now there was crowd of police officers and medical people filing in and out of Edge's apartment. There were several investigators and the Mayor was called. Inspector Hunnington was standing in the doorway of Edge's apartment in awe of the sight he was witnessing. He had no idea that John (Jack) would go this far as to kill an officer of the law. It was not his style. Edge was sitting in his recliner as Inspector Hunnington approached him and set his hand on his shoulder as to comfort him, the only way he was accustomed too. Edge looked up and stared at the inspector with anger in his eyes. He was not angry at the inspector, but at himself for letting this maniac slip through his fingers more than once. "I don't have the words . . . ." He was cut off by Edge, "Yea, I know Inspector; It's an empty feeling, isn't it?"

Charlie was still examining the body and moved the detectives head forward. He noticed a large hematoma on the back of his cranium from blunt force trauma. It seems the detective was hit with a blunt object first before his life was taken with the garrote. Charlie noted all his findings in the preliminary field report. The garrote was placed in an evidence collection bag and photographs were taken of the crime scene from many different angles. His weapon was still holstered as if he never knew what had hit him. There were no fingerprints anywhere outside of Edge's and Abbie's in the crime scene. The killer most likely wore gloves. There was arterial spray on the curtains and the floor surrounding the body. One shoe was off and lying in the living area, indicating the body was dragged to the chair. There was no sign of a struggle. This ended Charlie's investigation.

Edge knew it was his responsibility to inform the next of kin, since he did this a week ago with the dead girl on Goat Island. It was not a pleasant task, but since he was the senior detective in the squad, it was up to him. He got up and walked down the stairs to the cold outdoors, so Charlie could prepare Detective Reyes body for transport to the morgue. He walked to a bench on Third Street, sat down with the inspector next to him and offered the inspector a cigarette, which he accepted, and Edge flipped his Zippo until the inspector's was lit and then his own. The inspector drew a long drag of the cigarette and immediately began to cough heavily, since he was unaccustomed to smoking. Edge turned and grinned at him while his coughing fit was continuing. He finished his coughing fit with tears in his eyes and threw the remainder of the cigarette away in the street. Edge continued puffing away while looking up and down the street at the passing cars, all awhile the flashing lights of the emergency vehicles were still in front of his building.

Charlie didn't bag up Detective Reyes body; instead, he just placed it on an ambulance gurney with a white sheet over his face. He had to take his friend to the morgue and clean him up, so he would be presentable to the next of kin. Detective Reyes was married and had one child on the way. The ambulance attendants placed him in the ambulance and they were gone. Charlie noticed Edge and the inspector sitting on the bench and walked over to join them. "Hey! Charlie, all finished with the prelims? Do you want to go with me to visit Reyes's wife?" "Naw, I have to get back to him and make him look good for his wife's viewing. I hope you don't mind. How do you do it, Edge? I mean how do you keep your composure during this ordeal? I mean he was a friend of mine and all, but I don't think I could sit there and watch the reaction on his wife's face as you tell her that her husband isn't coming back anymore" Charlie kept on. "It's just part of the job Charlie, just part of the job," Edge responded.

Edge rose from the bench as Charlie walked to the CSI vehicle. He watched as Charlie was walking briskly wiping away the tears for his dead friend. He turned to the inspector, who was still seated and said "C'mon Inspector, let's go face his wife." The inspector got up and was following Edge to his car, and they got in and drove away, leaving the investigators still at his apartment to finish the minor details. Edge would have to find another place to stay since his place was now a crime scene. He would stay at Abbie's or at the station until he locates Abbie's whereabouts. He knew that John (Jack) had kidnapped her and would be holding her as a hostage. But where? He would figure that later since he was about to tell Reyes's wife the bad news.

They rolled up to the Reyes residence on Pear Avenue in the LaSalle district of the Falls and proceeded to the door. Edge knocked once and Maria Reyes opened the door and noticed the two Detectives at her front stoop. "Lieutenant Woodredge, how nice it is to see you. It's been a long time since we spoke," she said. "No it's not nice, Mrs. Reyes, we're here on business," he stopped and swallowed hard. Her smiling face diminished to one of concern. "May we come in ma'am?" Edge asked. The inspector stood motionless and continued looking at the ground. "Sure by all means, step in. What's going on? Is it my husband?" she asked looking at both of them. "Please tell me, is my husband been hurt?" tears were swelling up in her eyes. "Please sit down Mrs. Reyes, we have some bad news." Maria Reyes sat in her living room on the couch with Edge sitting next to her and the inspector across from them. "This is Inspector Hunnington from London. He is working with us on the ripper case. This is not easy for me but I have to tell that your husband has been killed this evening. We believe he was a ripper victim, but we're not confirming that just now," Edge looked away as Mrs. Reyes was crying uncontrollably on hearing this dreadful news. Edge didn't have the words to express his sympathies except to hold her as she cried.

Edge, Inspector Hunnington, and Maria Reyes arrived at the morgue. Charlie mort escorted the trio to the room where Detective Reyes lay in state. The sheet was pulled over to expose his face to his neckline. She had asked Edge if she could see her husband before he was taken to the funeral parlor. Charlie placed his arm around Maria as she still sobbed, and seeing her husband lying there was unbelievable to her sense of reality. Her sobs were heavier, the closer she came to his lifeless body. She nodded that she was ready to go, and as they left the room, Charlie's eyes were also filled with tears. Maria turned and looked at Charlie and uttered "Thank you." Charlie nodded back to her and she knew that if she needed anything, Charlie would be there for her. Edge and Inspector Hunnington drove Maria Reyes back to her Pear Avenue home. Edge walked her to the door. "Would you like me to send an officer over to keep you company?" he asked her in a soft voice. "No, Thank you, I have to call his mother and father and then I'm going to call my mother and she will come by and stay with me. My mother and I will make arrangements. Thank you so much for your kindness. Good-bye."

Chapter Twenty-Eight

Edge and Inspector Hunnington returned from the Reyes residence and were greeted in a crude fashion by Captain Eckersley. One of their own had been murdered and this latest was a top priority. Anytime a police officer dies in the line of duty, a manhunt ensues. Every officer was called in and a citywide manhunt was being conducted. No matter how small the clue would be, it was going to be checked out. Captain Eckersley approached Edge and Edge held up one finger as if to say . . . . "I'll be with you in a minute or not right now." Eckersley looked at Edge and knew this was not the time or the place to discuss the case. He knew Edge was hurted and very pissed off. He let Edge's slight insubordination slide for right now.

Edge sat down at his desk and pulled out a ciggy, not lighting it, since there was no smoking in the Detective's room. He peered over at Reyes's desk only to see an empty chair. He knew it wouldn't be empty for long. His thoughts were of Abbie and who might have taken her and where would she be. Inspector Hunnington was with Captain Eckersley in his office and Edge looked toward that direction only to see hands waving about and lips moving as if he were watching a silent movie. He noticed the captain looking at him but paid him no mind. He wasn't in the mood to deal with a managerial idiot. Everything Edge had done up to this point had to be cleared by the captain: no more clearances and no more permission. Edge was doing things his way from now on. If the inspector didn't like it, well, he could piss off back to London where he belongs. Edge knew 100% that John (Jack) had kidnapped Abbie and somehow had something to do with the murder of Detective Reyes. It was frustrating that one officer was dead and another's life was in jeopardy. He would find Abbie at any cost even if it meant his life instead of hers. He knew this wasn't going to be the case. It would be John's (Jack's) life and his carriage drivers.

Edge had read the fake story that his reporter friend Andy wrote the previous morning and it suited him just fine. Maybe John (Jack) had seen it also and it aggravated him into frenzy. Edge knew exactly how to get people pissed off with his sarcasm and his demeanor. John (Jack) wasn't any different. Edge's plan was ready to go with the pastors and the S.W.A.T. team on stand-by. He needed to protect Abbie at all costs. If his hunch was right, John (Jack) wouldn't harm her because he was infatuated with her for some unknown reason. Maybe it was her pretty face or her auburn hair or he just needed a hostage. What better hostage than someone Edge cared about or just a police officer. Whatever the reason, John (Jack) needed to make the next move.

John (Jack) had tied Abbie with a red scarf, hands behind her back and another red scarf for a gag to keep her mouth shut. He was pleased with his prize but not pleased with what happened to Detective Reyes. It was not his forte to kill Bobbies. He was not told at first that Angus had killed the Detective. He read the story in the daily newsprint. He had also read the story about the ripper case being closed and that did infuriate him to the extent to kidnap Abbie Cook. It was true that he did take a liking to her, but not for the purpose of killing her but for her graceful way of moving and her auburn hair. There was a mystique about her in which he admired, a different type of woman. She had spunk and liveliness. She wasn't afraid of him and he admired her for that. He was disappointed with Angus that he did not follow his instructions to the letter. He would deal with him later.

Edge had not eaten in a couple of days and had a few days growth of beard on his face. His hair was messy and he appeared to look homeless. His eyes had dark areas under both of them. He had not slept since Abbie's disappearance. He has taken a lot of heat from the captain, in which the captain has taken heat from the chief and the chief from the Mayor. As the captain has said many times, probably too many for Edge to count, that shit rolls down hill until it hits the bottom and splatters all over everybody. He laughs every time the captain says it because no one shits on Edge and gets away it. He showed what type of cop he was when he grabbed the judge and cuffed him at the dinner engagement with the mayor. It didn't bother him at all. He didn't feel a thing. The judge was humiliated and the mayor was embarrassed, but he didn't care. He needed the judge and he took him away. He's lucky, as Edge didn't book him for obstruction of justice. Edge reminisces on his finer moments. He tries Abbie's cell phone again, hoping to get answer but it just rings until her voice mail greeting comes on. Edge grabbed his camouflage coat and walked to the window of the captain's office where the inspector was still chatting with the skipper. He motioned with one hand for the inspector to leave the office. The inspector notices it and joins Edge on their way out of the squad room. "Where are we off to old chap? the inspector asks halfheartedly. "To get a beer," Edge retorts.

On their way to the British Pub, Edge had an impulse to cruise by Goat Island and check on the area where the battle would start against evil. It was getting late and he needed to relax but knew he wouldn't be able to knowing Abbie was out there somewhere with John. He arrived at the parking area where the river runs on three sides. There was a snowplow sitting off to one side and the parking lot was covered in snow except for an area just large enough to fit the carriage, not that it would arrive there but it was empty just the same. Edge got out of the car with the inspector standing at his half-open door. Edge walked around the area toward each side glancing at the various sides of the river, watching as the white water rushed in every direction. He was standing at the point he thought the vortex would open to allow John (Jack) to enter. He knew he wouldn't drive the streets of the Falls, since every police officer was on the lookout for him. He walked back to the car as the inspector was looking at him strangely, not understanding the full extent of Edge's mind. "Why are we here, Edge?" the inspector asked in a low quizzical tone. "Look about you. What do you see here?" Edge returned his question with a question. "I see a half snow-covered parking lot with a snow plow on the side," the inspector sounded half apologetically. "I see a battlefield and a victory," Edge grinned back. "It's getting pretty foggy out here and it's beginning to snow. In fact, the fog is coming in awful fast from the river, so I think it's time to hit the pub," the inspector said softly.

Edge got back into the car and sat there looking out the front windshield trying to see anything he could in the fog. It was getting pretty thick in the short time they had been there. "He's here, Inspector. I can sense his presence. I thought I saw a movement in the area cleared by the plow." Edge straining to see through the thickness. "I don't see anything yet Edge," Inspector Hunnington added. "Do you hear that, Inspector?. It's the sound of horses. I told you he was here." "I believe he has always been here, mate, since I didn't see any lightning strikes to open the vortex." "He must have been hiding real close to this area. I believe he wants to return with Abbie to his own time. But what does he want with her? He can't have her. She belongs to me."

They exited the car with their weapons at the ready and slowly moved toward the spot where Edge thought he saw the carriage moving slowly through the fog. They figured if Edge saw the carriage, then John (Jack) must have seen the headlamps of his car. The snow was blowing pretty steady now and was stinging their faces obscuring their vision. They proceeded cautiously trying to stay in the same direction, training their eyes to see through the fog. Their ears were straining against the sound of the wind, and the cold was invading their bones. The combination of their adrenalin and the chill of the weather were causing their hands to shake involuntarily. They stayed within sight of each other not to get separated far apart and get lost. They stayed silent as not to alert their nemesis.

They were getting close because Edge could hear snorting of the horses. Edge and Inspector Hunnington came up on the carriage and each took a side. They opened the carriage doors on an agreed silent count of three and peered inside as the snow was blowing a cross wind through the opened doors.

Edge noticed Abbie was tied up inside unconscious. He climbed in and began to untie his lady. He tried lightly slapping her on her face to revive her but was unsuccessful. She must have been under the arsenic effect. At the same time as Edge was trying to get Abbie to come too, Angus had jumped on the inspector from atop the carriage. Angus was on the inspector's back with a knife, trying to stab the inspector. The knife was glancing off the body armor that Edge had given the inspector prior to their departure. The inspector's weapon had been knocked out of his hand and was lost in the snow. The inspector was feeling around in the snow, so he could get the upper hand. Edge heard the scuffling on the other side and went through the carriage to assist his partner. Angus had the inspector on his stomach and was ready to plunge the blade into the inspector's throat as Edge put his 9 mm to the head of the driver. "Hey fuckhead, go ahead and give me a reason. I'll be glad to send your cheeky-ass back to the century you belong in as a ghost. Where's your boss? Matey," Edge asked. Angus felt the gun behind his head as the snow was continuing to bite his face. He stopped in midair and dropped the knife. Edge kicked him aside away from the inspector. Inspector Hunnington recovered and proceeded to cuff the driver when another voice interrupted him. "I wouldn't do that if I were you old chap" John (Jack) said smiling. Edge muttered "shit" and they both looked at John (Jack) who had a large knife held to the unconscious Abbie's throat. "Angus, get aboard," John (Jack) ordered. "I don't think so muffin cake," Edge said as he trained his s&w on Angus. The snow was stinging and it was difficult to see, even as close as they were. The blowing snow didn't seem to bother John (Jack) and he wouldn't hesitate to slice her throat. As Edge moved his gun toward John (Jack), Angus had stood and climbed aboard awaiting his master's next command. "Ah, ah, ah put the iron down Bobby or she will be my next work," John (Jack) pressed the knife deeper into her exposed flesh of her throat. Edge did what he was commanded to do and John (Jack) closed both doors to the carriage and tapped the roof of the carriage with his cane. That signaled Angus to drive away leaving Edge and Inspector Hunnington stunned again.

Chapter Twenty-Nine

Edge and Inspector Hunnington both stood there not believing what just happened. The inspector searched the area for his weapon, while Edge picked his up and brushed the snow off returning it to its holster on his hip. The snow had lightened a tad and Edge was helping the inspector locate his. After a short time Edge found the .38 special and gave it to Inspector Hunnington. They both ran to the car as they both noticed the lights through the fog. The car was still running and the heat never felt so good what little of it there was.

"I can't believe this shit," Edge commented as they both sat there befuddled at the event that just took place. "This asshole slipped away again. Well! He has to be around here someplace. He can't hide a carriage that size just anywhere." Edge rambled on. Inspector Hunnington listened tentatively as Edge continued, and he sounded angrier with each word. "May I interject here, old chap and may I say that getting angry at this point in time will do us no good. We must keep a level head. This monster does what he does best and that is the elusiveness of the law. He has been doing it a long time. He knows nothing of today's forensics. He lives on instinct and cunningness. He uses his environment and disguise," the inspector stopped as Edge held up his hand. "What the fuck are you talking about?" Edge asked with a more serious tone. "Forensics, elusiveness, cunningness. What the hell is that all about? This guy is an insane maniacal killer who hates women for some reason and I aim to take him out," Edge said with force in his voice. "But, he is a genius and survival is his main goal, not the destruction he is doing. Not the killing. It's all a part of the equation of survival. He needs to kill to survive. Understand." "Yes Inspector I get where you're coming from. I'm just concerned about Abbie. I need to get her back. She is not only a police officer, but a person whom I care a lot about and also is my friend," Edge said as he was finally calmed down. "Amazing! Lieutenant, you do have a sensitive side to your personality," the inspector said chuckling. "Hey Inspector! I have one comment for you. Fuck you and your sensitive side. Let's get the hell out of here and search for this a-hole.

Edge and the inspector drove down Buffalo Avenue in their police issue p.o.s. (piece of shit) with the defroster half working and ice and snow accumulating on the wipers and windshield. Edge had to stop and scrape the windows and clean the wipers even though the defroster was on high. The snow was still falling steadily and the fog was still present. The inspector said nothing as Edge drove slowly down the street looking as best they could at the vacant buildings lining both sides of the street. They came to the LaSalle section of the city and Edge decided to turn around since he figured John (Jack) couldn't have gotten this far in a horse and carriage without being seen by someone driving along this stretch of road.

John (Jack) had taken the carriage from Goat Island over the said bridge down Buffalo Avenue to Tenth Street where there was old warehouse just past the railroad viaduct. He busted the lock and lifted the overhead door and Angus drove in. There they would remain. The inspectors wouldn't think of looking for them in this place. The warehouse was large enough and seemed to be a storage facility. It had many crates and boxes piled on one another, a couple of old cars and antique furniture. An office was off to one side with a computer on the desk. John (Jack) stepped out of the carriage as Angus opened the door. They both looked around and were amazed at what they saw. "Strange isn't it? Angus. This century. I definitely belong here. There is so much work I can accomplish here. Don't you think my friend?" John (Jack) said with a smile. "Yes, my lord, but that was a close call not forgetting what had just happened on the island. I could have been shot again," Angus said in a worried tone. "Let's not dwell on that old chap and concentrate on our work. "Did you bring the Tea cakes when we left London?" John (Jack) asked. "Yes, my lord, I did and I brought some brandy also," Angus responded. "Good fellow, let us open the brandy and have a couple of tea cakes since our guest may be awakening soon and maybe hungry," John (Jack) ordered. Angus proceeded to the back of the carriage and opened the carriage box bringing out the brandy, tea cakes and a couple of brandy snifters for him and John (Jack).

Abbie had awoken from her drug induced stupor and looked out at John (Jack) and Angus having their brandy and tea cakes. She opened the carriage door and quietly stepped from the carriage crouching down not to be seen by the either of them. She was still a little groggy from the arsenic and took a couple of deep breaths to try to clear her head. The horses were ahead of her as she crept around the rear of the carriage being careful not to make any noise that would arouse or startle the horses. She stood there watching the two as they were engaged in conversation. It seemed John (Jack) was doing most of the talking. Angus was looking down at his snifter of brandy. Abbie was behind the carriage now and was looking at the overhead door. She looked around the building for a man door but did not see one. She knew by lifting the overhead door she would alarm the two and they would be on her in a flash, well Angus would, she didn't figure John (Jack) would even try. She left the cover of the carriage and quietly walked to the office door and tried the handle; it was her bad luck that it was locked. Abbie knew they would be checking on her shortly, so she had to find a place to hide. She needed a defensive plan and then an offensive plan to enable her escape. She managed to work her way to some stairs that led to a mezzanine with many boxes stored there. Maybe she would find a man door up there but she would have to be careful not to make any undo noise.

Angus's back was to her and John (Jack) was sitting on a crate that Angus had provided for him. John (Jack) was eating his tea cake slowly, while Angus had gobbled his down like he hadn't eaten a tea cake in a year. Abbie crept silently up the stairs on the seat of her pants keeping her eyes on the two as she moved one stair at a time. Her foot slipped on the edge of a step making a scraping sound and the duo were alerted when they heard the sound. She lay back on the stairs breathing slowly. Angus looked around the warehouse and up at the mezzanine but not at the stairs. "Rats, my lord," Angus said. John (Jack) nodded as if he agreed. A sigh of relief swept over her when she heard Angus say rats. She stayed there for what seemed like hours but was only a matter of a couple of minutes. Abbie made it to the top of the mezzanine; it was dark and much colder than the floor area. She moved among the boxes and crates and was startled by a manikin standing alone by the back wall but did not cry out. She didn't want to alert her captors of her whereabouts. Abbie couldn't chance using her pen light she carried around for they might see the light among the shadows of the warehouse. She worked her way to the far wall and found a man door and again tried the handle and again no luck. She was stuck in the mezzanine and it seemed the only way out was the overhead door down at floor level. She quietly moved back feeling her way around finding a fifty-five gallon drum. Opening the drum and then bringing out her pen light to check its contents. It was empty but smelled terribly of some kind of chemical. She climbed in and placing the lid over head. She was safe for time being in a smelly drum.

John (Jack) had finished his tea cake and brandy, got up from his crate, and went to the carriage to check on his guest. To his surprise, she was gone. He turned with a startled look at Angus and then looked around the warehouse. Angus looked at his master and he too looked around the warehouse as the expression on his master's face was puzzling. John (Jack) didn't have to tell Angus she was gone, Angus already knew by the startled look on his master's face. "Angus, you take the stairs and look for her and I'll take a look down here," John (Jack) commanded. Angus did what he was told and ran up the stairs looking between boxes and even checked the man door, then realizing it was locked, so she couldn't have gone that way. Angus left the mezzanine taking the same stairs stopping midway to listen for any movement or sounds from the area.

Abbie remained perfectly still in her barrel with her pen light still in her hand. The barrel had a terrible stench to it but it was the best cover she could find. She knew they were looking for her. She could hear Angus moving around the mezzanine moving boxes but he bypassed the barrel. She held her breath every time he came near the barrel. She was relieved he didn't think to look in the barrel. She didn't think he was that smart. So there she was stuck, her legs beginning to cramp slightly and the chemical smell was starting to make her light headed. Abbie remained calm and was listening to John (Jack) and Angus talking about her still being in the warehouse. John (Jack) seemed to be giving Angus a lot of orders and he was nervous as to which one to do first. Abbie lifted the lid slightly to try and get a glimpse of them. She noticed John (Jack) was standing between the carriage and the overhead door, while poor Angus was checking the floor level of the warehouse. John (Jack) looked up at the mezzanine and she quickly lowered the lid again and nervousness overcame her. She wasn't sure if he had seen her. She continued to sit there quiet.

Angus met John (Jack) by the carriage as he continued to look around scared because he was aware of what John (Jack) was capable of doing because of failure. He would blame it all on Angus. Angus needed another shot of brandy. "No sign of her, sir," as Angus was breathing heavily running around the warehouse. "I searched the whole place, my lord and not a stitch of her anywhere," he said with a worried look on his face. "The bloody wench has to be here my friend. There is no escape. The only door is this garage door. We will wait her out Angus. She will have to come out sooner or later. Time is on our side old fellow. Angus looked at John (Jack) and nodded in agreement with worried eyes. He knew John's (Jack) patience would wear thin and his frenzied look would appear and his wild tirade would start. Maybe if he could get his master to drink enough brandy, it would keep him from being too emotional and mellow him out a while. "Sir, would ye care for another spot of brandy?" Angus asked. "Yes, another spot would be nice my loyal friend.

Edge and the inspector were driving slowly down Portage Road under the viaduct and cruised right past the warehouse where Abbie was hiding from the terrible two. Edge turned his vehicle onto Mackenna Avenue to Nineteenth Street and then a right onto Nineteenth Street to the alley behind the warehouse. He parked and exited the vehicle. He proceeded to look around in all directions through the falling of the snow and the wind howling a bit as it had picked up blowing Edge's hair in all directions. He reached into his inside pocket and pulled out a pack of Camels, took one out and placed it between his lips, standing and listening for any sound he figured unusual for this time of year. What he was really listening for was the sounds of horses. He removed his Zippo lighter from his jeans pocket and attempted to light the Camel cigarette cupping his other hand over the flame feeling the heat. He stood there gazing around and in between directions taking a deep drag and blowing out the smoke watching it swirl around.

The inspector leaned partially out of the car door with his head between the door and the car. The wind catching his breath as he tried to yell to Edge. "Hey mate, what are waiting for?" Edge walked over to where Inspector Hunnington was sitting half in and half out of the car. "What are you babbling about over here, English muffin?" as was Edge's pet name for the inspector. "I was asking you what you were waiting for?" the inspector almost yelling into the wind. "The sounds of fricking silence" was Edge's reply. Edge flicked his cigarette out into the snow and got back into the car sitting there staring at the flesh colored warehouse. "It's the wee hours of the morning, Edge and we need to get some rest. Let us resume later on," the inspector added. "What do you think of that idea?" "I don't think much of it and I'm not all that tired. I'll drop you off and I'll go for a beer." Edge just sat there tapping his fingers on the steering wheel, his eyes in all directions as he had a strange feeling that Abbie was close to him. He looked at the inspector and started the car. The engine roared to life and they were off on the road again.

Abbie was trying to maneuver her position to get as comfortable as possible. The pain in her right hip was traveling down her thigh causing a cramp that she never felt before. Being as silent as possible, she shifted from her right butt cheek to her left, which alleviated some of the discomfort. She remembered she had a panic button on her cell phone, which would alert the police department to her whereabouts. She reached the cell phone holder only to find it empty. "Shoot-Fire she said to herself in a tiny whisper." She figured it must have fallen out when they abducted her. She would wait and see who would win the game of waiting each other out. She knew they would have to soon go back because the storm would be letting up. She lifted the lid of the drum a little to get a glimpse of John (Jack) and Angus. It seemed they were making rather merry with their drink. It wouldn't be too long now before they would leave. She lowered the lid and sat there in the confines of the drum thinking of Edge.

It was getting dark in the warehouse, probably darker than outside when John (Jack) ask Angus to light the lamps on the carriage. They were filled with oil in the bottom with a wick up through the base, one on each side of the carriage. Angus stood up and half staggered to the carriage arousing the horses a bit. "Easy boys, it's just me, Angus," as he stroked their manes and patted them on the neck. He opened the carriage door and under the seat was compartment he removed a box of matches, took a match out and struck the side of the carriage. The match lit immediately, cupping his hand over the flame, pulled the lever of the lamp raising the glass cover just enough to light the lamp. Both lamps now lit brightened the warehouse with ghostly shadows along the walls. "Haaa! That's quite a better sight. Now I can see what I'm drinking and maybe we can have a better look around here before we have to return. She is still here, my friend. I can smell her blood" John (Jack) said with an eerie smile. A smile that indicated he was ready to kill again. "May I speak, my lord?" Angus asked. "By all means, what's on your mind?" "Well, Sir, It's getting late and we must get back to stock up on provisions before we return, if we choose to do so," Angus's speech was becoming slurred as the brandy was taking its effect. "Let us search this awful place a last time and then we shall depart."

This time John (Jack) went up the stairs using his cane as leverage, twisting the handle and pulling out a long blade from the staff of the cane and began to stab various boxes. The wooden crates were sealed, so he knew she couldn't have hidden in any of those. He tapped his cane on the wooden railing and Angus looked up and noticed his master was motioning him to come up stairs. He hobbled up the stairs as best he could with the brandy still working on him. He stood next to John (Jack) as he was pointing at the drum. Angus lifted the lid of the drum and peered inside only to find Abbie looking up at him. Angus grabbed her by the hair, only to be slapped on the back with the staff of the cane. "Not by the hair Angus," John (Jack) ordered. "Apologies my lord" Angus said as the cane was about to come down again. Angus lifted her by the armpits and she stood up slowly, the cramps subsiding as her legs were getting used to the standing position again. "Get your filthy English paws off me as she tried to fight back only to have Angus put his arms around her in a reverse bearhug sort of hold. "Did you notice where you were? Did you ever wonder that you would escape from me? I ponder those answers would be no," John (Jack) said smiling. Angus dragged her in a backward motion toward the stairs as they left the mezzanine. Her heels digging into the wooden floor as she fought with Angus with his every step. John (Jack) was behind them smiling and twirling his cane. The effects of the chemical drum were still lingering in her system as she was being dragged and shoved in the carriage. She tried to get out the other door only to have John (Jack) standing on the other side. She tried screaming, but John (Jack) held his cane handled blade to her throat only to have her realize it was futile.

"My dear Abigail, I must confess that you are a feisty one. It's a good quality to have a whore like yourself provide a little spunk. How would you like to visit jolly ole England?" John (Jack) removed the blade from her throat so she could respond to his questions. "First of all, I'm not a whore and the answer to your last question is *Go to fucking hell!* You blimey English piece of shit." "I was beginning to like you because of your auburn hair, but since your responses were not to my liking I think I will just run you through with my blade and be done with you. As for going to hell, I imagine I will see you there, madam. Angus, hold her down and I will take care of her consciousness. She will fight no more. Angus did what his master commanded and climbed on top of Abigail Cook and held her head in both hands, enjoying the comfort of her body. He noticed a little arousal in his trousers and she could feel him also as she was trying to fight him off but he was too strong. John (Jack) took his snuff box out his vest pocket and placed a pinch in each of her nostrils. The drug acted quickly and again she in a nightmare state. He placed her in an upright position and sat next to her as Angus opened the overhead door, climbed back aboard, and grabbed the reins and with a yeeeaaah! Slapping the reins, the horses sped out of the warehouse back to the vortex.

Chapter Thirty

Capt. Arthur Eckersley had a meeting with Chief John Andersen and Mayor Patrick O'Leary at 1400 hours (2:00 p.m.) in the Mayors chambers at city hall concerning the progress in the ripper killings. The Mayor was getting pressure from the people and the press wanted a statement from anyone. Thank god, there weren't anymore murders since the fifth victim was discovered. Now they had a missing police detective to worry about. She had been missing about a week now with no answers to their questions from Lieutenant Woodredge. Captain Eckersley was getting impatient with his Lieutenant and was contemplating replacing him with someone else, possibly Detective Olivio. He would give Lieutenant Woodredge the benefit of the doubt and have him come in on this meeting also.

Lieutenant Woodredge was about to get a phone call when he and Inspector Hunnington walked into the squad room looking weather beaten and tired from lack of sleep and having a few beers. Edge was the worse of the two. They proceeded past Olivio and the empty desk of the late Detective Reyes. The other desks were occupied by other Detectives (RAC patrol) and they all looked up acknowledging the two as they passed by. They didn't hesitate and stop for any casual conversation with anyone, just continued to the captain's office. Everyone in the room saw the looks on their faces as they entered the skipper's office and slammed the door behind them.

Edge plopped his butt down in the chair in front of the captain's desk and glared at him while the inspector waited for the captain to offer him a seat. "Please sit Inspector," the captain motioned with his right hand. "Please fill me in on the progress of the ripper case and the abduction of one my detectives. Please tell me you have leads or better yet please tell me you have the ripper in custody. The inspectors head went to the floor while Edge continued to glare not saying a word. The captain looked at them and held out his hands in an upward sign and then crossed his arms. His patience was wearing thin by this time and finally broke the silence again. "If you're not going to fill me in then get the hell out of my office and my squad room until you have something to say," Eckersley's voice beginning to raise an octave higher. "Skipper, don't mess with me right now, I'm not in the mood for your non-sense. I've had a bitch of a night," Edge glaring at the captain with a killer look. The captain looked around his office, up at the ceiling before he responded to his subordinates comments. He glanced at the inspector and then in Edge's direction and took a deep breath before he continued. He opened his desk drawer and removed a bottle that said Tylenol, opened the cap and removed two tablets. After placing them in his mouth, he grabbed a glass of water from his desk and lifting it to his lips he swallowed the tabs.

"Do you have a headache? Sir," the inspector asked with a raspy whisper. "Yes Inspector, my headache happens to be sitting across from you at this moment." Edge went to get up from the chair and the captain pointed to the seat with authority and Edge sat back down not uttering a sound. The captain sat back with his head against the chair off to one side, contemplating what he was going to say. "Listen here fella's, this is the way it is and this is the way it's going to be, slamming the palm of his hand on the desk. The excuses are getting too old and the chief and the mayor want this case closed immediately. I want my detective back safe and sound. Do I make myself clear?" "Clear as Big Ben sounding at noon, sir," the inspector noted. Edge sat there his eyes rolling in his head pretending not to hear what the captain was saying to them. Edge was fuming because they were being chastised for not capturing John (Jack) and getting Abbie back, not for any lack of trying. They were busting their butts on this case and putting in many extra hours and the lack of sleep seemed to be taking its toll, especially on Lieutenant Woodredge. "I called you two in here because we have a meeting with the mayor and the chief in the mayor's office at 1400 hours. Comprendae?" They both nodded in agreement at what the captain was saying and understood the pressure they were under by the public outcry.

Edge closed his eyes with his arms folded and began to snore. The captain looked at the inspector and then at Edge. His head was tilted off to one side and he licked his lips as if he about to eat. The captain sat back in his chair with disbelief and the inspector just held out his hands as if to say "*Oh well*" with a wily little smile to his English face. He held up one finger to his lips in an Sssshhhh! motion as to tell the skipper not to wake the baby. Capt. Eckersley just shook his head. Edge continued to snore as the skipper and the inspector went to the coffee station and poured them a cup of hot java. Capt. Eckersley mixed his and went to take a sip as he peered into his office at Edge still snoozing. He looked around the squad room at a few empty desks as most of the detectives took for the hills when the skipper raised his voice. They didn't want any part of it when the skipper and Edge get into an argument. Sometimes they wonder how Edge gets away with the insubordination, but the skipper knows that Edge is Edge and a good detective and also he will get the results he is looking for.

Capt. Eckersley sipping his coffee and daydreaming about the first time he met Lieutenant Woodredge and his first impression was not a pleasant one. The day he reported for duty to relieve his predecessor, Edge had a suspect by the hair and was pulling him through the squad room to an interrogation room. He thought "Oh lord, this is a law suit" for sure. The suspect was so belligerent that Edge took what course of action needed to subdue the man and make him control his actions. It seemed that Edge didn't give it a second thought when it came to controlling the prisoners. He was stepping on that fine line between the civilized cop and the bad cop. Edge may have looked like the bad cop, but always turned out to be the good cop. He got results. His momentary daydream was interrupted by Inspector Hunnington. "Captain, are you all right, Sir?" "Yes, Inspector I'm fine, I was just in a historical daze." "Aaaahh! A daydream, Sir." "Well it turned into a nightmare in the middle of the day, Inspector. Get him up and out of my office. You two go to lunch and then get cleaned up and look presentable for the meeting with the mayor. Any questions? Inspector." "No Sir" was the reply as he walked away and re-entered the skipper's office to awaken his partner.

Inspector Hunnington tapped Lieutenant Woodredge on the shoulder and the Lieutenant was startled but awake as he rubbed his eyes and looked up at Inspector Hunnington. "Lucky for the captain it was you and not him that woke me. I might have popped him a good one. And I would have smiled as I did it." "You just zonked right out in that chair, my good fellow. Didn't take ya long." Edge continued to look at the inspector not saying a word, just listening to his English accent. "Com'on we have to go and get cleaned up for the meeting with the mayor in a few hours." "Screw that road apple eatin' S.O.B," Edge retorted with disgust. Edge got up and lazily walked out of the skipper's office and they both left walking past the captain who gave Edge a long look as he approached. Edge returned his own look along with an elbow tit to the captain. The captain was about to say something to him, but Edge's smile as he looked back made him think again.

Edge and the inspector got into the police cruiser, Edge inserted the key and turned the ignition switch and the engine sputtered as if it was going to stall, but yelled "Com'on you p.o.s." and the engine's sound seemed to run smoother. "Christ, even the motor car seems to listen to you, doesn't it?" "I know how to handle women Inspector. You see a, as you call it a motor car, is like a women, sometimes you have to be a little stern with them to get them to understand."The inspector looked a bit odd at him but what the heck, he hadn't met anyone quite like Edge since he came to America. He was a strange one, this fellow called Edge. He had his own way of going about his police work. He may be a bit unorthodox but he had an effective way doing the job. Edge was pulling up to the Quality Inn as the inspector was finishing his analysis of his partner in his own head. The brakes screeched and the vehicle came to a halt. The inspector opened the door and stepped one foot out, turned and held out his hand. Edge looked at it and clasped it his out of respect, being a fellow detective. "See you in a few hours old chap," he said with a smile. "OK, Cheeky fellow," Edge said with a shit eatin' grin. The inspector walked away and Edge drove off to his apartment. He never made it as he was detoured to the British Pub for his afternoon liquid lunch. He didn't care if he was on duty or not, he needed a few under his belt when he had dealings with the mayor.

He walked in and plopped his buttocks on the barstool and ordered the usual, nothing warm, always cold, foam headed beer. "How's the case coming along?" The barkeep asked Edge. "It ain't and get this candy-ass soccer off the boob-tube, will ya? Put some American football on." The barkeep changed the channel to English style football also known as Rugby. "How about this sport?" he motioned. "Anything but Soccer and Ballet," Edge grinned. "I don't like any sport where they don't use their hands. It seems too feminine if you ask me." "Well I ain't asking you mate, came a voice from the other end of the room. You'll put the Soccer back on or . . . ." "Or what" Edge shot back as he whirled around in his stool to notice a man sitting at a table in a dark corner of the pub. "Or I'll split your skull." The Man rose from his seat and approached Edge as now they were facing each other, the man noticed Edge's badge dangling from around his neck. "Excuse me constable, I don't want to tangle with any lawman while I'm in your wonderful country." The man's demeanor changed suddenly when he saw the badge. "Don't let this badge stop you from feeling Froggy," Edge removed the badge and set it on the bar. "That will be your trophy if you can get to it before I kick your English ass right out the door." "No problems here mates." The barkeep said trying to keep the atmosphere mellow. "This English muffin here has the problem. He likes candy-ass sports. He must be a cheeky fellow. The man now enraged at being called a cheeky fellow, his face turning a slight shade of red, being an embarrassed at what Edge had said started to walk away and then suddenly without warning lambasted Edge on the side of his head with a nice round house right landing flush on the cheekbone. Edge's head swung to the right as his right hand knocked over his beer. He looked down and shook the cobwebs from the hit he took and came back with a right upper cut of his own, sending the man reeling against the table from the direction in which he came. Blood was seeping from the man's lips as he sat against the table using the back of his hand to wipe the combination of saliva and blood from his chin. His beer was also empting from the bottle from which tipped over when he landed on the table.

The bar patron got up and stared at Edge not wanting anymore of this Soccer hating American. He walked toward Edge with outstretched arms palms forward. Shaking his head in disbelief that Edge had only hit him once, but once was enough. "Let me refresh your brew my good man." He sat next to Edge as he was replacing his badge from whence it came. "No' one has ever laid a lick like that on me before." He was looking at Edge and Edge didn't even acknowledge his sitting next to him. Edge grabbed the bottle of Bud and held it up to the man sitting next to him, "To the scrap we just had," he said. "Agreed, not much of a scrap, but a scrap it was." The bottles clinked together and they both started guzzling their beers until the Englishman set his down first and then Edge did the same. "So, what's your game, why are you here in town?" asked Edge. "I'm here to catch a serial killer. Inspector Abbernathy, Scotland Yard, pleasure to make your acquaintance, he held out his hand and Edge accepted the greeting with his own surprised look on his face. Lieutenant Woodredge, the Falls police department, both had firm grips. "What serial killer are you looking for?" "I'm here to seek out and capture Jack the Ripper" came his reply. Edge looked slightly surprised and made a facial expression, moving his lips as if to ask another question but chose not to.

"Well, good luck in your search, Inspector. I have to go meet with the mayor and have to pick up some baggage on the way. Thanks for the beer and the scrap, see ya around." Edge left the tavern and walked to his apartment, which was only a block or so away. He would have to remind himself to mention this Abernathy character to Hunnington. Inspector Abernathy waved a gentle so-long to Edge and returned to his business at hand. Edge went upstairs and let himself into the apartment walked to the icebox and removed two packs of Camel lights cigarettes, one for his pocket of his coat and one to open now. He tapped the pack of the box upside down to firm the tobacco in the box, opened it throwing the wrapper in the ashtray pausing as he placed a camel light between his lips and thinking about whom he had just met. He didn't know if this guy was for real or the beers he had just consumed were messing with head. Inspector Abernathy couldn't be here nor could he.

He picked the phone and dialed the Quality Inn's number and asked for Inspector Hunnington's room. The inspector was not in at the moment as he was probably waiting for Edge in the lobby. Edge placed the receiver back on its cradle and left the apartment returning to his car in front of the British Pub. He drove around the corner and parked in front of the Quality Inn awaiting his counterpart. Inspector Hunnington appeared a minute later and got into the waiting vehicle. "What took you so long Lieutenant? the inspector asked. "I had a scrap with one of your fellow members of Scotland Yard," Edge replied. "You don't say," as he was looking at Edge's cheek where Abernathy had connected with his round house right. "What was his name if I may ask?" "Inspector Abernathy," Edge said looking at him. "Do you know him?" "Yes, I do, but that's not possible," the inspector looked quizzically at Edge sitting across from him. "Keep going, I'm all ears Inspector," Edge's attention was riveted. “Inspector Abernathy was the detective on duty way back in the day when Jack the Ripper was killing in London. He couldn’t be here.” “Well, I met him and I hit him a good one and then we had a beer together. I just left him at the British Pub. Inspector Hunnington was amazed at what he was hearing. Somehow, Inspector Abernathy had come through the vortex seeking the same killer they were. “We’ll speak on this later.”

Chapter Thirty-One

At 1400 hours (2:00 p.m.) Mayor O'Leary and Captain Eckersley were sitting in the office at city hall awaiting Lieutenant Woodredge and Inspector Hunnington. As usual the Lieutenant was late. The Mayor looked at the captain with an impatient expression. "Does this Lieutenant of yours have a habit of being late to important meetings or is he just being facetious?" "He's probably doing it on purpose to be a pain in our ass, Mr. Mayor." "I see! Well I will wait a few more minutes and then I'll just get what info I can from you to give to the press. I need to keep them satisfied. You understand, don't you Captain?" "Yes, Mr. Mayor," the captain said almost apologetically.

No sooner did the words leave the Mayor's mouth did the Mayor's administrative assistant, which she liked to be called, came across the intercom that the two detectives were waiting in her office. The Mayor told her to send them in at once. Edge and Inspector Hunnington entered the Mayor's office and Edge dropped his butt in the chair without any acknowledgement of being asked to have a seat. Edge looked around the office, which he thought was rather drabby looking for a man of his certain distinction. The office was a plain white color with a nice size desk with a high back chair. In the high back chair sat the honorable Mayor O'Leary. Edge looked at the rather portly gentleman with Irish red hair and a moustache to match. A handle bar moustache at that. Edge began to chuckle and everyone in the room looked at him with strange expressions on their faces. "What's so funny? Uh! Uh! The Mayor was cut off by Captain Eckersley, who said, Mr. Mayor this is Lieutenant Woodredge and Inspector Hunnington of Scotland Yard. The Mayor held out his hand, in which the inspector grasped and shook. "Welcome to our fair city. I hope you have had an enjoyable stay since you have arrived." "I have, Sir," the inspector replied.

"So, let's get back to the funny, lieutenant, what's your problem?" The Mayor directed his question to Edge. "You are the funny one," Edge responded. "Lieutenant! the captain exclaimed. "This is the Mayor you're talking too." "Soooo! Fucking what! Am I supposed to be impressed?" Edge said still chuckling. "Show some respect to the Mayor." "Look it here, Skipper, I have better things to do than sit here with you dumb-asses, like get Abbie back and catch this John guy. So what is it that you want from us Mayor?" Edge asked him through the chuckle. "You're right lieutenant the Mayor said in his Irish accent. I need information and an update on the case." "OK, Mr. Mayor, here it is in a nut shell. We almost had this killer a few times, but he managed to elude us. Inspector Hunnington was almost killed by his maniacal driver. He seems to travel under the cover of fog and it seems no one can see him but us. We have every car on the street looking but no one has seen a trace of him but us. There is one other person who has seen him, but he is a drunken crackhead. He was a witness to one of the killings." "Do we have him in protective custody?" The Mayor asked. "No, he doesn't need to be, because the killer doesn't know about him. He wouldn't kill him anyway. He only kills women. I can find him anytime I want him.

"That's the scoop on what's going on and we will be going now so we can continue on where we need to go from here." Edge looked at the Mayor and then the captain. The Mayor appeared dumb founded at what he had just heard and held out his hands in dismay. "Do you have anything to add Inspector?" the captain asked. "No, that just about covers it, sir" came his reply. "If there is nothing else I need to know, then you two are dismissed and keep Captain Eckersley posted on any progress." The Irish Mayor said softly. Edge got up from the chair and gave a halfhearted salute with his right hand (middle finger sticking out) and walked out of the Mayor's office with a grin on his face, because he knew he hadn't heard the last of this meeting from Captain Eckersley. Old Twinkie boy himself.

The inspector followed behind Edge also smiling and shaking his head wondering how Edge gets away with the shenanigans with his superiors. Edge turned to the inspector as they were exiting city hall, "I'll leave them to their mindless conversation." The inspector just nodded in agreement as they were approaching the car. They both got into the car and Edge started the vehicle, again sputtering to get going. Edge cursed at it again and the engine coughed one time and finally started. "It amazes me, Lieutenant that you get away with these various phrases and insubordinate practices. What do you say my dear fellow?" "Well, I don't take any shit from anyone and I say what's on my mind and if they don't like it, well they can go to hell in a hand basket for all I care. Anything else your English ass is wondering about?" A silence fell over the inspector as he had no comment to that. "No! I didn't think so."

Edge put the car in drive and sped out of the parking lot on Main Street heading toward the Falls downtown area where he figured John (Jack) might show up. The snow had finally let up and the sun was trying to peek through the overcast sky. The streets were still snowed covered and it was suppose to be slow going, but Edge didn't believe in speed according weather and street conditions. The car was fish tailing wildly and Edge was having a time of his life driving erratically until the inspector motioned to him to slow it a little.

"What the matter, English muffin, are we a bit squeamish today?" Edge said grinning at him. "I'd like to arrive in one piece, if you don't mind, my friend." "There we go again using that statement "My Friend." Edge was in a very particular mood plus having a few brews in him, so his driving was as terrible as ever making the inspector a bit on the nervy side. They continued down Main Street until they reached Second Street, left on Second to the circle over the Goat Island Bridge to Goat Island. "Where are going?" the inspector asked. "First we are going to grab the all American meal and then we are going stake out this one area where I think John (Jack) may arrive tonight.

They arrived at Parks Police headquarters and Edge left the vehicle and walked briskly into the building returning a few moments later. He sat back into the seat and took a deep breath reached into his pocket for a Camel light cigarette placed one between his lips and lit up, much to the inspector's displeasure. "What did you go there for?" the inspector asked. "Professional courtesy between agencies, OK bloke? I want them boys to stay out of the way until I radio for their assistance. They agreed. Edge took a deep drag of his ciggy as the inspector cracked open his window. The cigarette smoke was filling the car. Edge put the in drive again and they headed to Crazy Andy's hot dog stand close to where they would be on stake out. "This is what I call the all-american meal." They exited the vehicle and walked over to the stand where they were greeted by Crazy Andy. He was a big man later in his years with a full head of gray hair but still had boyish look to his face. He was a retired police officer.

"Hey Edge," Crazy Andy yelled as he had seen him enter his establishment. Edge smiled a partial smile as Andy held out his hand. Edge took it in kind and they shook. "So whose is your partner? Edge was about to speak when the inspector interjected, "I'm Inspector Hunnington from Scotland Yard." Andy shook his hand also. "What's your pleasure today Edge? Chili cheese dog, kraut dog or just plain? Edge turned to the inspector," What's your pleasure, what do you want on your slider? "I think I will fancy what you have, Lieutenant." Edge looked at Andy and said he would have the usual. Edges usual was a foot-long dog with cheese wrapped in bacon and hot peppers and onions. Andy proceeded to prepare the foot longs and when he was finished he placed them in a cellophane wrap and dog carton. "There you are, gentlemen, two foot-long sliders. Care for a drink with those?" "Ya got any brewskis hidden behind that counter?" Edge asked him. "You know me, don't you Edge, you sly rascal." Andy handed Edge a cold Budweiser, but the inspector had declined to accept his opt out for a bottle of water because Crazy Andy's didn't serve hot tea.

The duo returned to the car, Edge already chopping down on his dog and had already opened the bud. He had downed half the bottle when he heard sort of a choking and coughing coming from the inspector as he had bit into the hot peppers not realizing the hotness of the peppers. Edge was laughing uncontrollably almost choking on the dog himself. "What's the matter Hunnungton, can't handle the heat?" Edge asked laughing. "It's a bit much; you know the peppers and all." the inspector said all red faced. The inspector was slapping his chest and waving his hand in front of his face trying to cool his mouth down. He quickly put the water bottle to his lips and began to drink as fast as he swallows. This did not help but only made it worse.

Edge finished his dog as the inspector proceeded to remove the peppers from his dog putting them into the dog holder. He quickly finished the beer and tossed the bottle into the back seat with it ending up on the floor. Edge had checked out a walkie-talkie at the parks police sub station to keep in contact with them and police HQ. He turned to channel one which would give him both agencies. He knew Capt. Eckersley would be standing by for any information that needed to be relayed or any orders that needed to be given. "Lieutenant Woodredge to Parks police, over." "Parks Police, Lieutenant Schaffer, go ahead." "Radio check" came Edge's reply. "Loud and clear" he answered back. "Lieutenant Woodredge to radio" "Go ahead Lieutenant" "Same for you sweetheart," he chuckled. "Loud and clear, Lieutenant and I am not your sweetheart" the sexy female dispatcher's voice sounded on the other end. "Stick to radio and F.C.C. (Federal communications commission) proper protocol," she sounded impatient.

The female dispatcher whose name was Vera did not like Edge at all. She thought him to be too vulgar and obnoxious. Disrespectful was also added to that list. Edge didn't care what she thought of him. He never missed a wink of sleep over what anyone thought of him. He got the job done and that's all that mattered to him. He drove the car as close to Terrapin Point as he could and parked. "This is where we walk Hunnington," he told the inspector. "I have been to this lovely place before. Do you think the killer will show up here?" "You bet your English ass I do." This the easiest access to what he needs most. The connection of the water falls and a wide clearing for his entrance to the vortex. This is odd to say but I think he will get his thunder and lightning tonight. It's just a gut feeling but that's what I feel. They walked over to the railing as dusk was settling upon them and Inspector Hunnington asked Edge about the priests and the ritual they were to perform. Edge explained to him that he didn't want any unnecessary civilians getting in the way in case there was a fire-fight (one way of course). He knew John (Jack) didn't carry any guns, but he wasn't sure about Abbie's weapon.

Edge leaned over the railing and let a big gob of spittle go and watched it as it sailed down into the falling water. He looked at the inspector as he had a strange look about his face. Edge told him it was a kid thing. The inspectors eyebrows lifted a little and that was good enough for him. Besides being a wise ass, he figured Edge had a little child in him also. They strolled over to the stairs and parked their butts in full view of the trail Edge thought that the carriage would come down. The inspector started to say something and Edge held up one hand to hush him up. "Listen, do you hear that roar?" he asked. "No, the inspector said. I only hear the sound of falling water." "It's rare this time of year but it does happen. Thunder when it begins to snow."

Snow was beginning to fall at a steady pace, big flakes. It was Christmas snow as Edge liked to have called it. This would be a slight nuisance but they would deal with it. Inspector Hunnington was used to the snow since they get some pretty mean snowstorms in London around this time. The thunder was moving in at a snails pace which would be to the duos advantage. A fog bank was also coming in from the falls and the direction in which they had their attention. "Lieutenant Woodredge to Parks Police and Capt. Eckersley, over" "Go ahead Lieutenant" Eckersley here. Parks Police sounded right after Capt. Eckersley. I'm at Terrapin Point and I need back-up. It's almost Showtime."

Capt. Eckersley jumped up and grabbed his overcoat throwing it on as he was leaving his office. He told Detective Olivio to follow and not ask any questions until they were in the car. They took the elevator to the underground garage and ran to the captain's parking space where a much fancier Ford sat waiting. The captain hit the remote button and opened the doors and held it longer as it started the engine also. They both got in and the captain put it in drive and turned on his cherry which was located on the front of the dashboard. He sped out of the parking garage and headed to Terrapin Point.

Parks Police were already stationed nearby as Edge had instructed them. He ordered Lieutenant Schaffer and his men to be at the ready but under no circumstances is there to be any shooting unless it was ordered by him. There were eight parks police officers counting the Lieutenant hidden at various points of the perimeter. They left one opening and that was where John (Jack) would ride down in his carriage. It was getting darker now and Edge wished the captain's fat ass would hurry up. Edge could hear the thunder getting louder and rain had begun to mix with the snow. Edge's eyes were open wide and moving all over the area. He noticed the street lamp was lit but didn't give off much light to the area. This was a good thing. The setting was just right for the occasion. Tonight was night he got Abbie back and sent John (Jack) either to his maker or what Edge known as hell.

Captain Eckersley finally arrived at Terrapin Point, parked next to Edge's p.o.s. The Parks Police vehicles were also there. Eckersley and Olivio ran down the path and met Edge and Inspector Hunnington. It was now midnight and the wait was on. "I have Parks Police covering the perimeter." Edge whispered to the captain. I called you down here so you could witness first hand what we have been chasing after these many weeks. The way I figure it this is the most secluded spot on the island. He has to go home tonight. He wants to take Abbie with him as his final trophy." "Okay Edge this is your show. You make the calls." the captain said softly.

Chapter Thirty-Two

It became 1:00 a.m., and then 2:00 a.m., with no sound of horses and carriage but only that of the waterfalls. Edge was beginning to have his doubts and the captain was getting impatient also. Edge checked his Mickey Mouse watch, which glowed in the dark and the time was 20 minutes past 2:00 a.m. Edge walked out into the clearing and stood there listening. The rain had eased a tad but the snow was still falling steadily. Edge looked up at the sky and the snow was hitting him directly in the face. He stuck his tongue out to catch the snowflakes. "What's he doing?" Eckersley asked Inspector Hunnington. "It's a kid thing" was his response. The captain just shook his head in disbelief and figured Edge knew what he was doing. Edge continued to scan the area and listen for any sound not accustomed to the area at this time of year. By this time Edge's eyes were acclimated to the darkness and he was staring down the pathway. A lone figure appeared to enter the clearing and was walking toward him. The closer he had gotten to Edge; he began to recognize him as Inspector Abernathy.

He donned a fedora type hat and wearing long brown overcoat, which was partially opened to reveal a British made revolver, in a shoulder holster. "How did you know we would be here at this particular spot?" Edge asked him. "I followed you here," he whispered. "I'm an Inspector, remember." "Follow me, I want you meet someone," Edge commanded. "I am unable to accommodate you on that my friend. I cannot come into contact with anyone from my country in this period of time. I mean anyone of the law enforcement stature. I hope you understand. I know you have an Inspector from Scotland Yard here with you, so I'll just make myself scarce and wait in the shadows. Believe me when I tell you this that Jack the Ripper is on his way here. He has your friend and she remains unharmed as long as you do the right thing. Stay out of my way." "No can do, bozo, this is my city and your in it and things are done my way or no way. Do you get that message?" Edge was stern in his voice and Abernathy nodded in agreement much to his displeasure. Abernathy walked away and Edge returned to his group.

"Who was that you were talking too, Edge? Captain Eckersley asked. "That was someone from a long time ago. He will not interfere with our plans." "That was Inspector Abernathy wasn't it Lieutenant?" Inspector Hunnington asked. Edge just looked at him with a concerned expression and then returned his attention to the trail. The thunder was closing in around them and Edge knew it would be almost showtime. Lightning followed and lit up the sky temporarily exposing their positions. Inspector Abernathy had positioned himself near the street lamp but like he said in the shadows.

Edge knew their positions would be compromised by the lightning, so he again walked out to the clearing. He peered through the darkness again straining his eyes to get any sign of a carriage or horses. He noticed a fog coming in and right away recognized this as a sign that John (Jack) was coming. He removed his 9 mm Smith and Wesson automatic from its holster and held it along his side partially obscured from view. "Com'on you son of a bitch and meet me mono-e-mono," he said to himself under his breath. The fog began to get closer and started to surround him. He could make out some partial images of a driver sitting atop a carriage. The Parks Police and the inspector and Captain couldn't see anything except the misty fog. It was that dense.

The fog was thick as pea soup and the captain was getting worried that Edge was in trouble. He proceeded to where he thought Edge might be, followed by Inspector Hunnington. "Lieutenant Woodredge, are you all right?" He said in a low whisper. They both had their weapons at the ready also. "Shut the hell up! Twinkie boy, he is almost here." Edge shot back. The captain heard that remark and knew Edge was fine. He also knew in which direction to walk since hearing Edge's voice. He could here what sounded like snorting and tried to gain some vision through the fog. He was a few feet of Edge and waited there with the inspector. They both looked in all directions for sounds above and beyond the roar of the thunder.

Edge listened also and then suddenly heard the phrase "Whoaaa! Coming from the driver of the carriage. The carriage stopped just short of his position. The horses snorted loudly and Edge heard the driver talking to John (Jack). "We're here, my lord" Angus had said. "I am well aware of that Angus and we are not alone." Was his master's reply. "There is a serious bloke standing in our way. Would you mind removing him for our good?" "Not at all, my lord." Angus jumped down from the carriage, grimacing a little from the wound he had received earlier started walking toward Edge. Edge saw Angus approaching fists clenched, raised his weapon and pointed it at Angus, "hold it right there fella or you will be worm food," Edge shouted. Angus stopped suddenly unclenching his fists as he saw Edge's weapon pointed at him. He wanted no part of it. "You in the carriage step out and let me see your hands," Edge commanded. John (Jack) opened the carriage door and he stepped out with his cane in front of him and both hands visible. The fog had slightly dissipated and Edge's visibility was not so obscured.

His weapon was trained on both of them as Angus had not moved a muscle since Edge had the drop on him. "Without that pistol you ain't shite gov'na." Angus told him. "Silence Angus, this bloke isn't toying with us." John (Jack) said musingly. "He's right Angie baby I'm not playing games. Angus made a step closer to Edge brandishing his blade; "I wouldn't if I were you; drop the knife." Angus stopped and placed the knife on the step of the carriage. He leaned his head slightly toward John (Jack) as if he was waiting for his master's next command. "You are both under arrest for the murders of five women and one police detective. Kidnapping is the lesser of the evils," Edge said smiling. "Well my good fellow, I believe you think you have upper hand but on the contrary I have what you seek. An auburn haired fair skin maiden in my carriage." John (Jack) then reached into the carriage and grabbed Detective Cook by the hair pulling her half way out as the rest of the police officers stood there stunned training their weapons even harder on the two.

Detective Cook was unconscious and John (Jack) let her dangle out of the carriage as he drew the tip of his cane and produced a long sword from its stemm. He held it to her throat. "Ease up matey or her artery will drain crimson on this newly fallen snow." John (Jack) commanded. Edge continued pointing his weapon in John's (Jack's) direction, but Captain Eckersley and Inspector Hunnington had lowered theirs slightly. The captain had motioned to the rest of the officers to do the same. Except for Inspector Abernathy, he didn't have a clear view of John (Jack), so he cautiously moved toward where Edge was standing. Once in position he noticed the blade at the women's throat he immediately lowered his at half of what it was.

The storm was at full force and the thunder was deafening. The lightning temporarily blinded everyone in the area. "Get aboard the carriage Angus and grab the reins," John (Jack) again commanded. Angus did what his master commanded grimacing again from the pain in his leg. He sat atop the carriage waiting for his master's next move. Edge stood there blinking his eyes several times between lightning strikes in the sky. "You're not going to win this time Jackie-boy," Edge said with a shit eating grin. "Yes, I know your real title but not your identity. You are Jack the Ripper." "Much obliged for the recognition my good man. I have to leave now. My work here is finished." As he was about to grab Detective Cook by the hair again, her eyes opened and she did a reverse somersault and rolled away from his attempt. Jack quickly jumped back into the carriage and shouted onward home to England to Angus. He reined the horses and shouted "Yeahhh! The horses reared back and the crown on the top of the carriage lit up as the lightning bolt had attracted it. Lightning hitting the crown causing a tremendous crack of thunder and sparks flying in all directions. The carriage was beginning to disappear. Edge commanded everyone to fire at the crown. Shots rang out from every direction, surrounding the carriage and the crown exploded as the carriage totally disappeared into the vortex. At the last possible moment Inspector Abernathy ran to the back of the carriage and jumped onto the back stand where the carriage box was. Jack the Ripper was gone.

The thunder and lightning storm was over and past them and the rain had also ceased. Everyone gathered in the clearing and looked toward the sky trying to figure out where the carriage went to. There was a rumbling of talk amongst the parks Police and Captain Eckersley looked at Edge and Inspector Hunnington. "I wouldn't have believed it if I didn't see it with my own eyes." He proceeded to walk away and then realized that Detective Cook was still lying in the snow. Edge was already over there tending to her. He picked her up in his arms and gave her a big kiss and hug. "Are you all right? He asked. She looked up and slapped him across the face lightly and replied "What took you so long you big oaf?" In return she gave him her own style of his shit eating grin. The captain smiled and Inspector Hunnington shook his head at the statement she had just said. "Where is Jack the Ripper?" She enquired. "We sent to where he belongs. *Oblivion*!" Edge said holding her tight as he could. Inspector Hunnington looked at her and said "Hopefully Hell; He will never be forgotten. "Yepper, Jackie-boy is what I call *History*!" Edge rambled on just glad to have Abbie back safe and sound. The group started walking back to the cars and Edge and Abbie were walking arms around each other when all of sudden Edge turned around and peered back at the clearing. "What's the matter Edge?" Abbie asked him. "I thought I heard something back there. It must be the mighty Niagara" Let's go get a beer.

Catch me if you can!

Edwards Brothers, Inc.
Thorofare, NJ USA
November 14, 2011